FUNDAMENTALS OF BIOLOGY

PART 1: INHERITANCE

PENNY REID

FUNDAMENTALS OF BIOLOGY

PART 1: INHERITANCE

PENNY REID

COPYRIGHT

DEDICATION

For all the science deniers. I honestly wouldn't have felt compelled to write this book without you.

CONTENT WARNINGS

If you are a science-denier, you don't want to read this book. Even though it was written because you exist, you'll likely feel personally attacked and offended by it.

Other content that may be concerning: discussion of the manosphere, mRNA vaccines, billionaires, revenge, adoption, bankruptcy, cancer, fraud, violence/assault, insomnia, sleepwalking, other sleep disorders, racism, and using food as a coping mechanism.

[1]

THE COMPOSITION AND CHEMISTRY
OF LIFE

Samantha

I opened the piece of mail in my hand and discovered it was a wedding invitation. To my own wedding.

Wait. Let me back up for a second.

It was just after midnight and I'd walked home from the lab, ducking under awnings and construction scaffolding and thinking that New York City must manufacture wind for the sole purpose of making my life difficult. Kaitlyn, my former roommate from undergrad and the only person who would pick up my call at this hour, kept me company as I dodged puddles. Collectively we were dissecting whether or not the TV show *Friends* had ever actually been funny.

"It's not that I think Chandler wasn't funny," Kaitlyn said, and I could hear the telltale babbling of her baby in the background as I unlocked the three dead bolts of my front door, "but he definitely pioneered the whole 'man-child who can't communicate with women' genre. And I resent him for that."

"Are you suggesting," I said, twisting my wrist, "that sitcoms bear some responsibility for Martin's emotional constipation?" Martin

Sandeke was her husband and basically a bully to everyone but her as far as I was concerned.

She snorted. "Martin's emotional constipation was definitely present in utero. Don't slander Chandler Bing like that."

"You named your baby after a sitcom character, and you expect me to not make the connection."

Kaitlyn paused, possibly switching boobs, possibly weighing the threat of my mockery. "We named him Joey because it was the only name we both didn't hate. And Joey is short for Joseph, which is a perfectly reasonable name. If you don't like the name, that's on you, Sam. You never suggested anything better."

I had, in fact, suggested at least a dozen better names, including but not limited to: Bartholomew, Snape, and Dr. Indiana Jones. Kaitlyn had summarily rejected them all. I suspected that when the baby reached object permanence, he'd resent her for it.

"You could have named him after me. Samantha's a perfect name for any child if you say it with confidence."

The baby made a squelching sound like he'd inhaled a portion of his mother's areola. "Okay, 'Sam,' I have to finish feeding your godson. Text me if you get home alive."

"I'm already home, and"—I lowered my voice to a whisper—"you have to admit that the pivot scene was funny."

"That was one scene! One scene in a million seasons."

"Good night, mamma," I whispered.

"Good night, gorgeous friend," she whispered.

The call ended and I was left with the warmth of Kaitlyn's concern to guide me into the dark hallway. My calves were still burning from the four flights of stairs as I used my cell phone's flashlight and tiptoed to my shared bedroom.

Both bedrooms were silent, but I recalled something about my roommate Diya being on a long hospital shift. Kendra, who shared the other bedroom with Nakita, was probably sleeping at her boyfriend's studio apartment, which was even smaller than ours but had the benefit of being a five-minute walk from her job at the Lower East Side's only vegan barbeque restaurant.

My stomach rumbled, so I padded into the kitchen, poured myself a glass of water, and stared into the fridge with the vague, quixotic hope that some new form of nutrition would have materialized in the past twelve hours. It hadn't. But a bag of expired shredded cheese glared back at me from the top shelf, accusatory and possibly sentient.

Abandoning hope of finding sustenance in the fridge, I quickly scarfed down a protein bar and washed it down with a glass of water. After flossing and brushing and doing the bare minimum of my skin-care routine, I finally made it to my room. I'd left the overhead light off, but the lamp atop my nightstand was on. A stack of mail sat on the center of my bed, presumably Kendra's passive-aggressive way of reminding me that I hadn't touched my basket of mail by the front door for the last two weeks.

That's when I spotted the envelope.

It was large, not quite cream colored, with elaborate calligraphy. There was gold foil. There was an actual wax seal. The front read, "Miss Samantha Jarlston" and had my address. I frowned, guessing it was an invitation to a wedding but wracking my brain trying to figure out who might be getting hitched. Slitting it open with the nearest sharp object, which happened to be my lab ID badge, inside I found the world's most excessive wedding invitation. The kind you had to hold with both hands, as substantive as an Amex Platinum card.

The honor of your presence
is requested
for the marriage of
Andreas Kristiansen
to
Samantha Jarlston
Saturday, June 19th, 7:00 PM
The Oslo Opera House
Oslo, Norway
Dinner & Dancing to Follow

I stared at it for a long, dumb second, then glanced around as if someone were filming my reaction. This was so random and weird.

I had not agreed to marry Andreas Kristiansen. I hadn't even spoken to him in over a decade. Actually, fifteen years and one month to be precise. The last time we saw each other, I'd been thirteen and numb. He'd been eleven, wearing an ill-fitting black suit, and crying into a bowl of fruit salad at my father's funeral.

This had to be a prank. Or maybe he was marrying someone with exactly my name? But then, why send me an invite? Or, more likely, this was a mind-game maneuver by the Kristiansen family to force me into a position where I would have to publicly acknowledge them or some such nonsense. I still received requests for interviews about the events surrounding my father's disgraceful downfall and death, even now, and even though I'd never given a single one.

The Kristiansens were shady as a forest, but they had more money than the devil. I wasn't stupid. As much as I wanted to see them all burn in hell, I wasn't going to cross them without equivalent financial backing, or rock-solid evidence, or both. Realistically, the closest I would ever get to revenge against that family would be to ignore their existence, let them think I might someday give an interview that would tank their company's stock, and live as well as possible.

Basically, I didn't want anything to do with them unless it meant reading their obituaries.

I tossed the invitation into the trash and, for the second time that night, reached for my phone. There was a text from Diya ("I'll be home in the morning") and a missed call from a New York City area code I didn't recognize. I ignored both and started to compose a ranting text message to Kaitlyn, only to stare at the screen for two minutes, and then delete it. There were limits to our friendship. She had a baby who she'd purposefully named Joey. Clearly, she was dealing with a lot right now. I didn't want to bother her with this nonsense.

Crawling under the covers fully clothed, I tried to sleep but my brain performed an elaborate postmortem on every interaction I'd ever had with Andreas Kristiansen.

Andreas was two years younger than me, and he was the kind of child prodigy that other prodigies resented on principle. He was fluent in three languages by eight—but, to be fair, his mother was Italian, his father Norwegian, and he spent summers in the USA—and the kid played chess like he'd been born with every possible opening, middle game, and ending hardcoded in his DNA.

His father, Oskar, had been my dad's business partner and, eventually, one of the people who'd bankrupted and then destroyed my family (according to my mother). I don't want to dwell on that part—if you spend fourteen years in therapy, you learn to summarize childhood trauma in one sentence or less—but suffice it to say, I had zero interest in sharing my last name with anyone in the Kristiansen bloodline. The invitation was absolute nonsense. Like, Mad Hatter nonsense.

Still, Andreas had always been . . . different. And not in a bad way. Not at all.

I'd spent my childhood summers at his family's Hamptons house, where the two older Kristiansen boys ignored me in favor of their wild-oats sowing. However, Andreas followed me around with the intensity of a golden retriever, always asking questions, always eager to play. He was sweet and curious, once getting so invested in building a blanket fort that he convinced their housekeeper to sew custom curtains for the windows. When he was nine, he found a dead baby bird in their garden and wept for a full hour, insisting on holding a proper funeral with eulogies and everything.

I was the officiant, naturally. Because I'm eloquent and look fabulous in robes.

He was lean and pale and had this thick, chaotic mop of dark hair that made him look like an extra from a Tim Burton movie. And, if you weren't used to it, his gaze was intense and intimidating. There was something about the color of his olive-green irises and the shape of his large eyes, something about how his lids naturally drooped when he was in a state of concentration, listening, or rest that made him appear both bored and belligerent, like he was just about to give you a judgmental, unimpressed slow blink.

Almost ten years ago, while doomscrolling, I'd stumbled across a news article about him. According to a reputable British newspaper, he'd become a six-foot-two chess demigod and the second youngest grand master in Europe's history. Also, he was a vegan at sixteen. Which, to be clear, is not an insult *at all*, but I was generally suspicious of anyone who forgoes cheese by choice. That's an inhuman amount of self-control.

There'd also been a relatively famous meme about him and his intimidating stare. It was a photo of a teenage Andreas looking at an opponent across a chessboard, and in bold white text outlined in black it read, "My mouth may not say it, but my face definitely will."

That was the last I'd heard of Andreas Kristiansen until, suddenly, out of absolutely nowhere, and after not hearing from him for years, he reached out to me last month.

I didn't hear from him personally. He reached out through his assistant. *But of course.*

I'd been ignoring the emails from his personal assistant since the first one arrived thirty days ago. They always contained the same message, just with slightly different wording.

Mr. Kristiansen requests a half hour of your time to discuss a private matter.

Mr. Kristiansen requests that I reach out to arrange a brief meeting.

Mr. Kristiansen is in town and would like to meet you for a half hour to discuss something urgent and sensitive in nature.

At first, I suspected that he wanted to make amends for our parents' war, but the more I thought about it, the less I cared. He might've been something like a best friend to me when we were younger, but he'd grown up as a Kristiansen. Since I had no power or means to annihilate them, my life was just fine without reopening that chapter. Better to pretend they—all of them—didn't exist.

Then, two weeks ago, I was leaving the building where my lab was housed, and a stranger approached me with a slim manila envelope and a practiced smile. He introduced himself as "the personal assistant to Mr. Kristiansen" and asked if I could open my calendar to schedule a mutually agreeable meeting time. I told him the only arrangement I was interested in was a restraining order, and then I walked directly to the nearest pizza shop and stress-ate two slices of mushroom, cheese, and extra pepperoni.

But now, side-eying the invitation in my trash can, I realized that the situation had mutated. What began as passive pursuit was now full-tilt campaign. The Kristiansens had upped the ante. There was a calligraphed RSVP card with gold leaf embossed detail. There were flight vouchers. There was a slip of paper printed with a New York City phone number, and underneath it, two sentences:

Samantha, please give me half an hour of your time. If you don't want to talk or see me again after that, then I'll leave you alone. — Andreas

I wanted to crumple the card, burn it, toss it out the window into the East River.

My phone vibrated with a new text, pulling me out of my violent musings.

Kaitlyn: Did you think of any other funny episodes or scenes?

I typed back: "Not yet. But if I'm kidnapped, it's the Norwegians. Will explain later."

I placed the phone on the nightstand, turned off the light, and rolled onto my back, letting the city's ambient glow seep through the window and bathe my face in blue. Outside, a siren wailed, insistent and urgent.

I lay there for a long time, thinking about the last time I held a wedding invitation in my hands. Grandpa's second marriage. The memory made my stomach hurt.

I wondered if there was any universe in which I could RSVP no to my own arranged marriage. Probably not since I hadn't even been proposed to.

Eventually, I got up, fished the card from the trash, and ran my thumb over the embossed letters. I didn't recognize the font, but I liked how it looped, the swirls, the softness. Then, I studied the note from Andreas, presumably in his own handwriting. His cursive was sharp and tidy. It was nice, but it was aggressive, like a handshake from a man who thinks handshakes are tests of strength.

And as I stared at the points and lines of the black ink script on the thick ecru card, I couldn't help but think, *What the hell kind of person does something like this?*

[2]

INTRODUCTION TO THE CELL AND CELL MEMBRANE

Samantha

The sound that woke me was the ancient creak of our apartment's front door, followed by the telltale thud of a person surrendering their entire body weight onto the entryway rug. I groaned into my pillow and checked my phone: 5:33 AM. I'd fallen asleep a little after 2:00, which meant I was running a solid deficit on cognitive function and would need to supplement with at least two pharmaceutical-grade quad-shot Americanos.

There was a scrabble of keys, a sigh, and then the shuffle-shuffle of sneakers. Diya. Even before she creaked open our bedroom door, I could smell the ghost of antiseptic that always trailed her home from the ER.

"Samantha?" she whispered, voice raw from twelve hours of telling drunk NYU kids that their insides would stay inside if they'd simply stop doing shots for five goddamn minutes.

I rolled over, exposing my face to the icy air, and grunted. "In the flesh. What's up?"

Diya poked her head in. Even in the dark, I could see the reverse raccoon marks from her safety goggles. "Sorry I woke you," she said, genuine remorse in her tone. "I think I'm just so tired, I'm confused. I keep telling myself not to talk, and here I am, still talking."

"S'okay." I turned and buried my face into my pillow, letting it muffle my next words. "I should get up. I should get up. I should get up."

Motivated by the power of self-talk, I sat up in bed and cracked my eyes open.

Already removing her scrubs as she crossed the room, Diya tossed them into the laundry basket with one hand. She'd mastered the art of undressing without ever being technically naked; a hoodie materialized over her tank top before the scrubs even hit the basket. "You should go back to sleep. It's not even six."

"I'd have to fall asleep for that to work," I said, and then yawned. I knew myself and my terrible relationship with insomnia enough to know more sleep was now impossible. "I'll just get up and go to the lab early."

Diya grunted and plopped onto my desk chair. "Why am I sitting here?"

"You need a shower and you don't want to get in bed until you're clean," I filled in.

Diya let out a tragic sigh and blearily blinked around the room. "But the bathroom is so far away."

Her eyes drifted, but then she did a double take, frowning at something on my nightstand. I followed her line of sight and cringed. Our early-morning, sleep-deprived repartee would now be derailed by the bright, accusatory rectangle of the wedding invitation on my nightstand. I could see in the dance of her dark eyebrows on her forehead the train of her thoughts.

"What's that?" she asked, tilting her head. "Are you getting married?"

"It's junk mail." I snatched it from the nightstand and folded it in half. "You're hallucinating. Take a shower. Go to sleep. Dream of your mom's rogan josh."

"No, no. I know myself. I don't start hallucinating until I've been up for seventy-two hours. That was your name on there. Who is the guy? Is it the Stanford guy? I hate that guy. Or the one who did Cross-Fit? Please tell me it's the CrossFit guy, I miss his shirtless sleepovers. Oh! The lawyer guy, the one you went to law school with who keeps making us dinner. Or the rower? Eric? Is that his name?"

"None of those," I said, shoving the folded invite into my backpack on the floor next to my bed, where it could no longer radiate weirdness throughout my personal space. "Just an old family fri—" I stopped myself from saying *friend*. He might've been my friend when we were little, but we were strangers now. And, obviously, no one else in his family had ever been a friend to me. "Someone I used to know playing a joke."

Diya made a skeptical face but let it go. Apparently, she was too tired to chase the scent of gossip.

"I'm heading out early," I said, flipping back my covers. "Have a project due and the sequencer is actually free before eight."

She nodded, her head tilting back as she succumbed to a massive yawn.

Standing, I hunted around my room and threw on the least-wrinkled pair of jeans I could find, a Genetics Bowl Champion tee, and a cardigan that might've been trendy seven years ago but now existed solely to telegraph "harmless grad student" to the outside world. I finger-combed my hair into a haphazard bun and grabbed my bag. Leaving Diya to her dozing, I washed my face, brushed my teeth, and called it good.

After I put on my coat and slung the backpack over one shoulder, I caught my reflection in the mirror by the front door. When I was on the tennis team in undergrad, I'd been told a few times that I resembled a young Anna Kournikova, the infamous Russian tennis pro. This was back when I worked out daily, was outside in the sun often, and still dyed my hair blond. I definitely preferred the light brown of my hair color now. My thoughts must've still been preoccupied by that stupid fake wedding invitation because, in my quick assessment of my reflection, my brain told me I looked like someone who could plausibly be a mail-order bride, but only if the groom had specified "bargain bin, will not arrive as advertised."

The thought made me snicker.

Yes, yes. Make it all a joke. Everything is a joke. Life is so much nicer that way.

* * *

By 6:00 AM, the city was running on three-quarters power. I could actually enjoy a sidewalk without having to weave through a marathon of tourists and startup founders on electric scooters. The air was crisp, and even though I could see my breath, I left my hands exposed. The summer had been so hot, I was still enjoying the cooler temperatures of fall.

Central Grounds, my favorite coffee shop, operated on the theory that coffee should taste like coffee and be better than good. The line was mercifully nonexistent, and this small win buoyed my mood.

My barista—Kevin to his friends and regulars—smiled sympathetically when he saw me. "Rough night?"

"You have no idea," I said, rubbing at my temples. "Quad-shot Americano, please."

"On the house if you can recite the Krebs cycle backward."

I blinked. "You know I can."

"I know you can, but I want to see if you can do it before coffee."

"Fine," I said. "Malate, fumarate, succinate, succinyl-CoA, alpha-ketoglutarate, isocitrate, citrate, oxaloacetate." I stopped for a second. "Wait. I started with malate. That's not—"

"Impressive enough," he said, waving it off. "Nobody ever gets that far."

I grinned, because it felt good to be a monster at something.

He slid the coffee across the counter with a nod of respect. "Make good decisions."

"I shan't." I tipped him, grabbed the drink, and inhaled it.

Ah. Coffee.

I loved coffee so much. I'd always liked coffee, but now I loved coffee. It was likely the closest I would ever come to a committed relationship.

Armed with my favorite thing on earth, I beelined for my department building. The NYC campus was close to the university's research hospital, a collection of structures cobbled together by whatever real estate happened to be available during the dot-com crash. The genetics building, my home for the next indefinite period of time, was a neoclassical monstrosity complete with white columns made of cement and fairly decent scrollwork, considering the building was less than one hundred years old.

Gulping the last of my coffee, I would've been perfectly content to marinate in my own productivity until noon. But as I turned onto the sidewalk, an unusual sight pinged my situational awareness. A new stranger—a genuinely remarkable-looking fella—leaned against one of the entrance columns with an aura of extreme confidence. He wore an obscenely nice tan overcoat. The kind you see in European cologne ads, probably cashmere. It was unbuttoned and therefore open, revealing his all-black attire beneath. Black turtleneck, black pants, and black shoes shined to a mirror finish. Unlike mine, his hands were ensconced in leather gloves.

Currently, he checked his phone, then pocketed it and stared straight ahead. If this were an undergrad psych experiment where one rated an individual's attractiveness on a Likert scale, I'd have categorized him as "dangerous levels of hot." So, a 5.

The part of myself that was still somewhat aware of my outward appearance wished I'd brushed my hair this morning. Hell, I wished I'd done literally anything other than roll out of bed and slap on the first clean-ish T-shirt I found. But . . . whatever. Who cared if Mr. European Perfume Ad saw me looking like this. We'd probably never encounter each other again.

Squaring my shoulders, I adjusted my bag and told myself not to get distracted. I had things to do, data to analyze, coffee to drink. I was making for the door, eyes fixed on my phone screen as I pulled up my email, when he stepped directly into my path.

I glanced up. He looked at me. I took a step back. He kept looking at me.

So, the stepping in my path wasn't an accident. It was calculated. He'd measured the trajectory and plotted an intercept.

My heart, which had coasted along inertly for the better part of a year, spiked a little.

"Pardon me," he said.

Nice voice. Very nice. Low and smooth, with a faint European inflection that I couldn't pin down but absolutely believed got him laid on a regular basis.

I blinked at him, then did the New Yorker thing where you make yourself so unimpressed that it comes back around to seeming interested.

"Yes?"

"You're Samantha, yes?" He cocked his head, his green eyes sweeping over my face. The man's tone broadcasted interest, but his gaze seemed somehow both bored and intense.

I took another step back, scrutinizing him, and considered pretending I wasn't Samantha, but the way he'd pronounced my name, dragging the *a* out ever so slightly, made me want to engage rather than lie outright. "Depends. Who's asking?"

He smiled, and it was a micro-expressive thing, barely more than a twitch at the corners of his mouth. "Andreas Kristiansen. You got my note, yes?"

It took my tired brain a full second to realize that this wasn't just some random European thirst trap. This was *that* Andreas, the youngest Kristiansen, the boy—no, the man—who'd sent me a wedding invite and put himself as the groom. And when it did, my heart tripped all over itself and I stood paralyzed for several long seconds, chasing my breath.

I had no idea if he noticed or was bothered by my sleep-deprived gaping. Andreas simply stood there and returned my stare, giving me time to collect myself, as though he'd foreseen this reaction to his sudden appearance after fifteen years.

By the time I'd collected myself enough to respond, I was breathing hard and my heart had taken off at a gallop. I cycled through every available response and landed on the most mature by far. "I'm busy."

He didn't seem offended. Good for him.

"You remember me," he said, sounding certain and pleased, though his expression didn't change.

I didn't respond. I owed him nothing. Also, I didn't know what to say or why my body had suddenly divorced itself from my mind.

After studying me for another long moment, he gathered a deep breath and glanced over my shoulder. "It's urgent that we meet."

I spoke without thinking. "So, you show up at my job?"

His attention cut back to mine and he gave me another of his micro smiles. "Despite the risk, I suspected waiting for you here would be more efficient than waiting for you to answer an email. Or a letter. Or a courier."

I laughed, once, because it was either that or throw my empty coffee cup at him. "I was hoping the next step would be a singing telegram. Or a skywriter." Again, I'd spoken on instinct, the sarcasm emerging without thought. His sudden presence had sent me into a panic and I didn't understand why.

Andreas's face flickered with what might have been amusement, hard to tell. "If there'd been time, I would've done that next."

I glared at him while also suddenly very aware of his proximity. He didn't smell like cologne, but there was a faint, unfamiliar trace of something herbal and clean. Like rosemary and ozone, like the air after a thunderstorm, if that's even possible.

Clinging to sarcasm like a shield, I made no attempt to hide the largeness or loudness of my sigh and took yet another step away, outside of the radius of his seductive olfactory assault. "What do you want?"

His gaze darted past me, scanning, then fixed on my face. "May I buy you a coffee? Or is that redundant?"

The fact that his voice was so incredibly alluring irritated me. I looked at my cup of coffee, which I'd just finished, then back at Andreas, intending to turn him down.

Thus, no one was more surprised than me when what came out was, "Fine."

"Thank you," he said, sounding sincerely grateful, gaze moving over my face like he was hungry for the sight of it. My eyes narrowed.

What are you doing, Samantha? This feels dangerous. Don't do it!

Clearing my throat, I added testily, "If you promise to leave me alone after, then fine. I shall go get a cup of coffee and listen to whatever you have to say."

If my glare bothered him, he didn't make any outward sign of it, instead saying, "There is a café just there. I believe they opened at six." He lifted his hand toward the corner across the street. "We can talk for a bit, and—"

"No." I turned and began marching toward the café he'd indicated, not waiting to see if he'd follow. "You said in your note a half hour would suffice. I'll give you a half hour. And that's it."

[3]

CELL INTERIOR AND FUNCTION

Samantha

We sat across from each other, a table's width and fifteen years of silence between us. I picked at the sleeve of my cardigan, which had sprouted a new hole at the elbow I hadn't noticed until now, and wished I'd insisted on meeting somewhere less . . . sterile.

Cafés were supposed to be neutral ground, but this one had only fake plants. Who can trust a café where every plant is fake? What else is fake? The beans? The tea leaves? The milk? Is the barista made of cake?

I'm just saying.

Andreas looked even more beautiful with prolonged exposure, in the uncanny way that only comes from a ruthless culling of childhood awkwardness. His features had all grown into themselves. The nose was still prominent, but now it belonged on a man instead of a scrawny middle school student. The jawline could cut diamonds, and the choco-late-brown hair, which had once lived in perpetual revolt, was mostly tamed and combed with a kind of clinical precision that made my scalp itch with sympathy. The only thing unchanged was his eyes. Large, round, olive green, and weirdly soulful for a twenty-six-year-old nepo baby.

When I initially spotted him earlier, I'd thought that his eyes were rather large, yet he must've been tired or bored or something similar because his eyelids were lowered, at half-mast. But now I recalled this quality to his gaze—the appearance of drooping eyelids, as though he were unimpressed with everything—was just part of his eyes' natural shape.

Presently, Andreas stared at me, silent and perfectly still, save for the gentle motion of one foot, which tapped against the marble tile in some intricate tempo I couldn't decipher.

I was immediately viscerally annoyed.

"So," I said, after exactly enough time had passed for the silence to become an entity with its own mortgage, "are you going to say something, or is this some kind of strategic interrogation?"

Andreas blinked, startled out of whatever he'd been thinking. "I haven't seen you in fifteen years. I'm curious."

"Curious?" I repeated, incredulous. "Did your family hope I'd be in a ditch somewhere? Preferably not breathing, I suppose."

His eyes narrowed slightly, but he didn't dignify that with a response, instead continuing to stare at me with a level of focus that left me unsettled. I wondered when and why his family had decided to use him to make contact. I wondered, not for the first time, why I'd agreed to this.

But I also wondered if he still wept for baby birds; I wondered if he still built pillow forts; and I wondered whose bed he slept in when he had nightmares.

Summers when we were young, he used to climb in my bed whenever he had a bad dream. This was almost every night. We'd stay together until early morning, then he'd leave silently so as not to be found out.

But that was a long time ago.

My attention wandered, eventually moving to the espresso machine behind the counter as I longed for the nutty, robust taste of the coffee I'd finished earlier. The server—an androgynous twentysomething with sleeve tattoos and a septum ring—caught my eye and smirked. Andreas had ordered us two cappuccinos when we'd entered. I raised my eyebrows at the server and didn't smile, in the universal expression for "please save me from this torture," and they nodded, presumably recognizing my desperation.

After too many seconds to count, during which Andreas continued to stare and I felt increasingly like something under a microscope, I snapped, "What is it?" If I didn't take control, Andreas was going to benzodiazepine me into a coma. "You asked for half an hour. That's two percent of my day if I round for scientific digits and don't count leap seconds. I need a return on my investment."

As though deciding something, he leaned forward, elbows on the table, hands folded with priestly solemnity. "I did not want to meet you in person like this, not in public. But you left me with no other choice."

"Why? What? Are you still mad at me for hiding that puzzle piece when we were little?" I looked him down, then up. "Are you going to throw a pie in my face? Is it humble? Will I be expected to eat it?"

"I want to marry you."

I choked so hard that I fleetingly worried I would aspirate on my own tongue. "Excuse me?" I finally croaked out.

He didn't blink. "The offer is sincere."

"I—" For the second time in less than twelve hours, I looked around to see if there was a hidden camera, but no one jumped out of the faux foliage. "Andreas, I haven't seen you since we were both preteens. You can't just—What is wrong with you?"

He seemed unbothered by the fact that he'd just detonated the world's most awkward and inappropriate proposal. "You asked what I wanted. I told you. I want to marry you."

Before I could formulate a reply, the server arrived with two cappuccinos, each topped with a foamy heart. I was ninety percent sure this was not a standard design, and ten percent sure the barista was flirting with Andreas.

Yes. Please. Take him off my hands.

But I only said, "Thank you."

After a brief exchange during which the server confirmed we were all set, they left. Andreas, meanwhile, didn't even nod or otherwise acknowledge the café employee. He simply kept looking at me.

I waited until the server was out of earshot before continuing. "Did your family put you up to this? Is this damage control for the sake of shareholders before something new about my father comes out?"

Andreas shook his head. "I don't associate with my family. I haven't since I turned eighteen."

"Then you're here on your own." I side-eyed him, deciding that if he said so, I would believe him. Maybe that made me stupid, but I didn't think so.

Andreas's childhood hadn't been easy, and I got a sense that it had continued to be difficult after I'd disappeared from his life.

Confirming my statement, he nodded. "This is something I want. They do not know I am here, and if they did, they definitely would not approve."

I stared at his beautiful face for several seconds, trying to wrap my mind around what he might be thinking with this random, out-of-the-blue proposal after fifteen years of no contact.

Eventually, I huffed. "Seriously, is this some kind of performance art? Do you need a green card? Is there a reality show I'm not aware of for world's most uncomfortable reunions? Why are you doing this to me?"

The faintest hint of a smile barely curved his lips. "You have not changed," he said, the words sounding tender.

My adrenaline spiked and I sipped the cappuccino just to have something to do. It was good. Not great, but a credible effort.

"Okay, so—why—" I floundered, unsure why I hadn't picked up my bag and coat and left already. Old time's sake, maybe? "Let's say, for the sake of argument, that I don't immediately tell you to get lost. Why would you want to marry me?"

Eyes narrowing, he tugged at the fingertips of his gloves—first the right, then the left—proceeding to pull the black leather from his hands, revealing long, thick fingers and finely formed knuckles, every-thing strong, veiny, smooth, and perfectly proportioned.

I squirmed, viscerally annoyed once more. Andreas had one of the finest sets of man-hands I'd ever seen in my life. *Infuriating.*

Rather than roll my eyes, I frowned. I definitely needed to get out more, go to a bar, find a nice set of hands for a night. At the very least, I needed some time off work and my dissertation when I wasn't exhausted, time to take care of my dearth in sexy-times business myself. Things must've been desperate if I was noticing my sworn enemy's hands.

He is not your enemy. He never has been.

That said, this—sitting across from him now—was *hard.* Just seeing him was difficult. Talking to him brought back too many memories.

My mother, when I was little, before she'd died, had said that Andreas preferred me over his own family and she'd always felt a little guilty at the end of every summer when we'd have to part—him for Norway, then almost immediately for school in Switzerland, and me for school in Connecticut. He'd cry like he'd never see me again and I'd feel melancholy for weeks.

At my father's funeral, Andreas had refused to let me go, requiring four grown men to untangle his arms from my body and forcibly carry him away. I would never forget his tearstained face and how his hands reached for me. At thirteen, I'd been in no state to console him, since my dad had—you know—just died right after declaring bankruptcy. I had no home, and my mother had been a shell, and every day was a struggle.

Over the years, every time I thought about reaching out to Andreas, some new hellish event stopped me: my mother's death, my grandparents' divorce, my grandmother's death.

When I looked Andreas up ten years ago, just before starting college, he was the best chess player in the world and seemed to be doing just fine. And so, I'd let go of my childhood friend once and for all. It had brought me closure. I'd never regretted it.

But looking at him now and his bonkers offer, maybe he hadn't let go of me . . . ?

That's nuts. It's been fifteen years.

Ignorant as to the direction of my thoughts, Andreas reached into the inner pocket of his coat and produced a document. He slid it across the table with the same gravity one uses to reveal a murder weapon in a game of Clue.

I glanced at it, then at him. "What is this?"

"Just read it."

Careful to avoid touching his perfect fingers, I picked up the page. It was a photocopy, not an original, and the English was so precisely translated that it felt unnatural. The letterhead said Genetix, Inc., and the footer was dated approximately one month ago. The rest was legalese, but the gist was unmistakable.

Upon my death, my shares in GENETIX INC. shall be transferred not to my biological children, but to my first grandchild, regardless of gender or national origin. The shares shall not be held in trust by any Kristiansen, Aaberg, or Loretto relation until such time as the grandchild reaches the age of majority.

I read it twice, noting that Aaberg was the maiden name of Oskar Kristiansen's first wife and Loretto was the surname of his second wife. Finished, I set the paper down.

"Whose will is this?" I asked, but I already knew.

"My father's," Andreas said.

I tried to swallow around the tightness in my throat. "Oskar is still alive?"

He nodded.

"That's a shame. Do your brothers know about this part of his will?"

"No."

Blinking against a sudden rush of tears, I huffed again, then snorted, hoping to dispel the stupid, tiresome liquid emotion. "What does any of this have to do with me or you wanting to marry me?"

I needed to get out of here. *Feelings* were clawing at my lungs, heart, and throat, which was not a sensation I enjoyed. Ever.

He met my gaze, unflinching. "Those shares should go to you. Or your mother."

I felt my throat tighten further. "My mother died when I was fourteen, Andreas. Bit late for inheritance games."

He tilted his head, and for a second, I thought he might say something normal, like "I'm sorry" or "That must have been hard."

Instead, he went for the jugular. "I believe my father—and, in part, my brothers—they are the reason your father died. I believe either my father or Tobias defrauded the company and framed your father for it. Henrik helped them cover it up. That stress led to your father's sudden death."

The words hung in the air like a chemical spill, but they also helped me, centered me. When the old familiar numbness threatened, I embraced it. Breathing deeply, I looked down at my hands, then at the table, then at the page of the will, then back at Andreas, who was the picture of unruffled patience.

I swallowed without difficulty. "You think I don't know that?" I sounded so detached, so calm. *What a relief.*

He frowned at my response, another micro expression. "Samantha, I need to make it right for you."

"And marrying me is your solution?" Admittedly, I was only half listening to his words now, and I was definitely not in a state of mind to scrutinize them.

He nodded, like he was agreeing to a flavor of yogurt, not a life-altering commitment. "My father is very sick. He will not have a chance to change this again. If we marry, the shares pass to our child. You will control them. Don't you see? It's built into the language. My father wants his future daughter-in-law to control the shares before the child comes of age, to ensure either me or my brothers only marry someone trustworthy, ideally someone we're in love with." Andreas paused here, dipping his head and watching me as though to gauge my reaction to his words.

When I continued meeting his searching stare blankly, he sighed and added, "No need for me to sign anything over since I am a Kristiansen. The shares, and the company, will be yours to control from the start."

We gazed at each other silently for so long that the little foam hearts floating above our coffees began to blur. I tried to imagine any scenario in which this was a normal, sane offer, and came up empty.

"You want to have a baby with me," I said, slow and deliberate, "so you can keep Genetix out of the hands of your brothers."

"Not for me." Andreas's tone sounded gentle, so at odds with his cold beauty. "For you. For your family. Your father built that company. The patents, the technology, those were his."

I pushed the photocopy back across the table and lied, "I don't care about Genetix. Or your father's dirty money. Or any of this."

The intensity of his already-intimidating stare multiplied. "If you walk away, the shares will eventually go to one of my half brothers. Henrik, or Tobias. They will not hesitate to get married and have a child in order to control the company, or try to. You remember what they were like. They have not changed."

I did remember. Henrik liked to punch Andreas and call it wrestling. Tobias once superglued my hair to a piano bench. I had not kept in touch. Thus, I didn't know what havoc they'd wreaked since growing to maturity. To label them both bullies would be a charitable understatement.

Andreas must have perceived my indecision, because he leaned forward, voice dipping low. "You deserve your father's company. Not them, not me, not my father. You're getting a PhD in genetics, just like your parents. There has to be a reason for that. I'm offering you a chance to take back what should be yours by birthright. Why say no?"

I shook my head, suddenly exhausted, and not just from lack of sleep.

Yes, I would do almost anything to screw over his family and I'd gladly watch them suffer, but I wasn't completely morally bankrupt. I wouldn't involve an innocent—my own child—as a means to an end. That was some next-level evil strategic bullshit.

"I'm not bringing a child into the world just to spite your family and take control of a company. I would never do that."

He reached across the table and placed his hand on mine, his big palm completely dwarfing my fingers, and I flinched at the feel of it, yet was unable to pull away. The contact was warm and electric. It paralyzed me. A tingling heat coursed up my arm and my breath turned to fire in my lungs. My body's unexpected reaction to his touch threatened to incinerate the blanket of numbness I'd been clinging to, and that was unacceptable.

"You don't ever have to see my family." He squeezed my fingers in a way that felt insistent and familiar. Comfortable and yet also alarming. "I would not let them near you. Trust me, Samantha."

"That's not the point," I croaked out, because—maybe it made me irrational—but I did trust Andreas. Careful to keep my voice just above a whisper, I said, "The mere idea of conceiving a child out of spite, especially with you, is loathsome"—I didn't miss how he winced, or how his eyes dropped to the table, but I wasn't finished—"to me. How could I do that? How could you even suggest it?"

His shoulders rose and fell, and his attention remained on the table as he added, "You don't have to see me after, if you prefer. We can arrange everything in writing."

Now I flinched, his words felt like a slap.

I found I had to swallow several times to gain control of my voice before I could trust myself to speak. "By 'after,' you mean after we are married and conceive a baby. Isn't that right? Are you telling me you want to have a child with me and then disappear from my life, from our baby's life?" While I spoke, I glanced at his hand covering mine, then at him, then back at his hand. I needed to pull away.

Any minute now.

Andreas's eyes cut to mine. He stared at me, giving none of his thoughts away. Or maybe he was giving his thoughts away. Perhaps he was broadcasting them loudly, but I couldn't read them, or him. I felt too many things I didn't usually allow myself to feel. And I was sleep-deprived. I couldn't think.

Finally, heart hammering, I pulled my hand back. I felt the loss of his touch and our contact in a way I dared not analyze.

"Exactly," I said, deciding to assume his silent stare meant that he would not, in fact, feel perfectly at peace with never knowing his own kid. Cupping my cappuccino, I didn't lift it for a sip. My hands felt unsteady. "I appreciate the offer to conspire to bring down your family, but no."

Face unreadable, his gaze shifted to some point over my shoulder. "This can be the beginning of the conversation. We don't have to decide anything right now."

Exhaling a humorless laugh, I set the cup down with a clatter and stood up, shoving my chair back with more force than necessary. It was well past time for me to leave.

"No. This isn't the beginning of anything."

He also stood. "Samantha—"

"You need to let it go." I looked around for my belongings, anywhere but at him, and wrapped my scarf around my neck even though my chest felt hot and achy.

"I cannot let you go, or let this go. The company should be yours."

I shrugged, still not looking at him. "Yeah, and people shouldn't be starving or unhoused in first world countries, marine animals shouldn't be choking on plastic, babies shouldn't be dying of preventable diseases, but neither you nor I can fix the inherent unfairness of life."

Andreas walked around the table and stood in front of me, his hands fisted at his sides. I could feel his restraint as though it were a tangible thing.

"Please, if I find another way, may I call you? May I—"

Yanking on my coat, I cut him off. "Sure. If you find a way that doesn't involve us getting married or having a baby together, be my guest."

"Wait." He grabbed and held my wrist, pausing until I—unenthusiastically—gave him my eyes. For once, his didn't look bored. They were wide and imploring. "If either Tobias or Henrik contact you, you must let me know. You have my number. Call me."

No. No way. I had no desire to relive this level of emotional upheaval. Not ever.

Disentangling myself from his grip, I shook my head again, firmer this time. "You won't be hearing from me."

"Sama—"

"Please. Leave me alone. Okay?" I hated that my voice wavered and cracked, but I seemed to no longer have control over my vocal cords.

Thankfully, Andreas made no move to grab me again. He didn't say another word. But I felt his eyes on me as I gathered my things, walked around him, and fled the café. My heart and lungs hurt, as if they were encased in rubber bands.

Feelings are THE WORST!

Outside, the cold felt bracing. I stood on the sidewalk, eyes stinging, lungs burning, and realized that I had never, in all my years of therapy, been this profoundly unsettled by a single conversation. I walked back to my department building. My hands shook, so I stuffed them in the pockets of my jacket. My stomach felt sour, and my mouth tasted bitter. And I had a headache.

I tried to convince myself sleep deprivation was the culprit, but even I didn't buy it.

[4]

METABOLISM OVERVIEW AND ENZYMES

Samantha

I spent the rest of the morning in a state of low-level dissociation, the kind where you run experiments and pipette reagents with the slow, sputtering detachment of a glitching DNA sequencer whose firmware is three updates behind. Perhaps it was my lack of sleep, but every time I thought about Andreas's offer to be my baby daddy, or his attempt at a hostile marriage takeover, or *him* in general, I spent no less than fifteen minutes staring into space and thinking about his face or his hands or his eyes, and reliving our moments together this morning before I caught myself.

Another side effect of Andreas's unexpected visit was the reemergence of my burning hatred for his family. I'd tried to forget, but the best I'd managed was letting go of my childhood in its entirety, like those years were a kite caught in a windstorm and the only way to be free was to let go of the string. For some reason, I couldn't seem to pick and choose which parts of my past to hold on to. At eighteen, I'd decided to throw it all away and start afresh.

But now here I was, marinating in the injustice of it all, how they'd stolen my father's company and ruined my family . . .

Then I'd blink and come back to myself in the present. Basically, I'd never been more grateful for the monotonous rituals of the lab.

My research project—my baby, my nemesis, the thing keeping me from sleeping, socializing, or remembering to send good friends happy birthday texts—was bioremediation of ocean plastics via genetically modified microbes. If you find that impressive, don't. There are lots of scientists trying to do the exact same thing.

Basically, if I could convince the right microorganism to eat the right plastic, and not, say, eat the entire aquatic ecosystem along with it or excrete hazardous toxins as biowaste, we might be one step closer to saving the planet's oceans before they became one giant floating land-fill. My day-to-day reality involved mutating a microbe that could, under strictly controlled conditions, dissolve polyethylene like it was fondue cheese. Getting it to do so in an actual marine environment, without triggering a new bubonic plague, was the tricky part.

Today I was running a third (or maybe fourth, I'd lost count) pass at sequencing some candidate plasmids to see if yesterday's late-night gamble with the CRISPR kit had stuck. It had, in that the bacteria were very much alive and very much eating the control plastics at an alarming rate. It hadn't, in that every organism that I'd genetically modified was now a different, nightmarishly resistant superbug that would likely haunt my dreams for the rest of the semester.

This was why our entire floor had security—badge access and state-of-the-art cameras—and even the offices were off-limits to anyone who didn't have a PhD in genetics, hope to have a PhD in genetics, collaborate with a PhD in genetics, or work for someone with a PhD in genetics.

I'd almost convinced myself that this latest failed attempt was merely another important datapoint in my research journey when a knock at the glass wall of my cubicle startled me into an upright posture.

Dr. James Nieminen stood there, perfect posture, perfect jawline, even his glasses were so clear and free of fingerprints I suspected he changed them out for a new pair daily. Unlike most of the assistant professors, who either dressed in "I'm hoping for tenure" cargo shorts or "I'm hip and relevant" hoodies, Nieminen wore business casual. He was the only person I knew who could make a button-down shirt look like a tactical garment.

I forced a polite, if not particularly sincere, smile.

"Hey, Sam," James said, lingering in the doorway. I didn't miss the way his gaze moved down to my chest, then up. "You got a second?"

"Sure," I said, even though I really didn't. And I didn't know what he hoped to get a glimpse of by checking out the vicinity of my boobs. I currently wore scrubs and a lab coat, having changed out of my T-shirt and jeans when I arrived. Perhaps this was just a habit for him with all women. He never did this to men.

Nieminen leaned against the doorframe, arms crossed, his stubby fingers gripping his elbows, and smiled the kind of smile you only saw on toothpaste commercials. "How's the ocean plastic project going?"

"Swimmingly," I deadpanned, then regretted the pun. "I'm making incremental progress. One day closer to creating an organism that will save the world, or at least delay the heat death of the oceans by a few fiscal quarters."

He laughed a little too loudly. "That's great, that's great. I always say, if the world doesn't appreciate the subtlety of your genetic engineering jokes, they deserve the microplastics." He laughed again, even louder.

I nodded, even though . . . *what did that even mean?*

James lingered, shifting his weight from one foot to the other. "So, hey, I was just wondering, are you going to the department holiday party this year?"

It was the beginning of November. "The one in, like, December?"

"Yeah! It's never too early to plan." He ran a hand through his dark hair, the movement calculated for maximum effect to show off his bulging biceps in his short-sleeve shirt, but my attention affixed to his hand. The palm was entirely too big for the size of his fingers. "Last year was such a blast. I thought maybe we could go together."

Blinking away from his disproportionate digits and up to his face, I floundered for an excuse.

I had nothing against James personally other than a mild sense of dislike. He was, objectively, smart and very good-looking, and he had the kind of research budget that made junior grad students swoon. But I'd never seen him be particularly kind to anyone unless he wanted something from them.

And, maybe this was me just being petty, but he'd interrupted my lab meeting last spring to debate the etymology of the word *pseudogene* in such a way that I'm pretty sure he expected me to remove my pants on the spot. The memory still left a bad taste in my mouth.

More importantly, James had a not-insignificant probability of being on my dissertation panel next year, and my entire academic future would be at his mercy for at least another twelve months.

Presently, I played it as cool as possible. "Oh, you know, I haven't really thought that far ahead. December feels very theoretical to me right now."

James grinned, undeterred. "I get that. You're very focused. It's what I admire about you. But you should come. Let loose a little. We'll go together." At the last minute, he lifted his hands. "Just as friends. No pressure."

No pressure, I repeated in my head, feeling as if I'd heard the phrase at least one million times in my life. "I'll think about it."

He took a step inside, lowering his voice like he was about to share state secrets. "You know, if you ever want to talk about your research, or anything really, my door is always open. Especially now that I finally got rid of my last postdoc. She was a total drama queen, you know? But you're different than other women. You're very mature."

"Thanks," I said, deserving of an Olympic medal for not cringing.

Ladies, beware men who tell you things like, "You're different" or "You're very mature." If a man says you're different from or more mature than other women, then he's just insulted either all women or you. And neither makes him attractive.

He smiled again, showing all his teeth, and I wondered if he'd practiced that in the mirror. "Great! So, I'll see you around, Sam."

I nodded, saying nothing.

He left, and I exhaled a long-suffering sigh. Returning to my notes, I did my best to concentrate, but my frustrations about Andreas's visit and his evil family and the unfairness of my parents' fates were now intermingled with the aftertaste of James's cologne, which was some mix of spearmint and musk that *lingered*.

Actually, it loitered.

Less than five minutes passed before a familiar voice floated over the partition.

"Are you hiding from Dr. Nieminen?"

I spun in my chair to see Dmitry Bortnik, fellow grad student and unintentional expert in the art of the slow approach. Dmitry was a year ahead of me, a Russian expatriate with high cheekbones and the kind of unhurried confidence that made him the natural enemy of all horny straight-male assistant professors.

"Not hiding," I said. "Strategically waiting until he's distracted by someone else's pheromones."

Dmitry snorted, then ducked into my cubicle, balancing a mug of something black and tarry with long, elegant fingers. "He talks about you all the time, you know. In the grad student lounge. Says you have 'the most graceful pipetting hands' he's ever seen."

"Gross," I muttered, but I was also a tiny bit pleased. As a hand aficionado, I never turned down a compliment about my hands.

Okay. Fine. Yes. I have a hand kink. I admit it.

I'd always been a hand woman. Some women liked eyes, some butts, some biceps, still others forearms, smiles, thighs, or six-packs. Not me. I loved me some well-proportioned man-hands. The kind I could imagine on my body, the kind that could grab fistfuls of me without any part spilling over.

I also took ridiculously good care of my own hands and owned a paraffin wax machine because I couldn't afford manicures but refused to have dry cuticles.

Dmitry grinned. "He's not wrong, though. You have good hands. Very steady."

"Stop." I tried to play it off, waving his words away, but I blushed. Obviously, I'd never told Dmitry about my hand fetish, so these compliments were hitting a bullseye he didn't know existed.

"Fine, fine." He perched on my desk, ignoring the pile of ungraded quizzes I'd been using as a coaster. "You look terrible, by the way. Trouble sleeping?"

I considered for a moment. My interaction with Andreas earlier today flashed through my mind. I knew Dmitry didn't mean to be offensive nor did I take his comment about me looking terrible that way. He was simply painfully direct and didn't have any interest in me as woman. Neither of us were interested in messing around with colleagues or orgasming where we ate.

Eventually, I nodded. "Something like that."

He raised his eyebrows, waiting for elaboration, but I was not about to unspool my entire morning with Andreas Kristiansen and his offer of transactional matrimony and baby making, or my body's completely bizzarro overreaction to seeing him again.

Instead, I focused on the safer, nerdier topics.

"Ever just . . . get the feeling your work is completely pointless?" I asked.

Dmitry sipped his coffee, then shrugged. "All the time. Especially when I see the latest paper from the MIT group. They are always three months ahead, no matter what I do."

"Those nerds." I punched the palm of my hand with a fist. "They clobber us in innovation, but we could totally take them in a fistfight."

He laughed, then softened. "If it makes you feel better, Nieminen will probably be suspended before your dissertation defense. I don't think he even understands what the postdocs do in his lab and I've heard murmurs from the grants oversight department that there's a problem with his expense reports."

"That does make me feel better, actually. Thanks." Perpetually turning down an assistant professor's romantic overtures was almost as dangerous as dating one. If Nieminen were suspended, then I'd breathe easier.

Dmitry's phone vibrated. He checked it, face going neutral. "My PI needs me. Don't let Nieminen bully you into going to the party. In fact, say you have a boyfriend. He might back off."

"Will you pretend to be my boyfriend, Dmitry?" I flapped my eyelashes at him.

"No," he said, and promptly disappeared, leaving behind a faint aroma of cigarette smoke.

I looked back at my notes, but the ability to focus had completely deserted me. Despite my best efforts, my brain continued replaying the morning's meeting with Andreas on a loop, refusing to let me rest.

Andreas Kristiansen wanted to marry me.

No. Correction, Andreas Kristiansen wanted to marry me and have a baby with me and then . . . ? He clearly had no idea and hadn't thought about what would happen next. The entire plan was so diabolically nonsensical. I would have to ask Kaitlyn if her uber-rich husband had ever proposed something as diabolically nonsensical. *Why are rich people so weird?*

Even worse, a not-insignificant, totally mortifying part of me— likely the part that hadn't gotten laid in over a year—was curious about what would happen if I said yes. Would we actually get married? Would he move in? Would we have to cohabitate and share a bathroom? Or would it be like a one-night stand, only with way more paperwork and the potential for a trust fund baby?

Even worser, that same part of me did not hate the idea of a one-night stand with Andreas. I was a living, breathing, straight woman after all.

Thankfully, a much larger part shied away from the idea like a teenage virgin faced with her first erection.

Andreas felt . . . scary. To me. His presence in my life felt volatile, like two bacteria competing with each other via pathogen signals. I wasn't afraid of Andreas. I knew he'd never hurt me on purpose and cared about me deeply, even now. But I also was afraid of Andreas, because he'd never hurt me on purpose and apparently cared about me deeply, even now. And how did any of that make sense?

Or maybe he doesn't care deeply about you at all. Maybe he cares about injustice, and this is all just about righting a wrong . . . ?

Ugh. I wished I'd gotten more sleep last night.

Regardless, I made a mental note to do an internet search for "Who is currently the best chess player in the world?" For now, I had to escape this lab before Nieminen returned with his weird tiny fingers, or before I fell asleep on my desk.

Grabbing my notes, I headed for the lockers, determined to spend the rest of the day doing something other than staring at my laptop. Maybe I'd go to the library and peruse the new fiction titles, pretending I had time to read them. Or maybe the bagel shop down the street. Or maybe a sensory deprivation tank, if I could sneak into the psychology building undetected.

Anything to stop thinking about the reprehensible Kristiansens.

And anything to avoid thinking about Andreas Kristiansen, and why I couldn't stop thinking about him.

* * *

I took the long way home, which is to say, I walked an extra ten minutes in the opposite direction of my apartment, just for the pleasure of existing outside in the cold. The sun had started to set, painting the sky directly overhead in orange and pink. It had been too long since I'd been outside at this hour.

The wind was up, and the temperature had dropped ten degrees since I'd last stepped outside, but I kept my hands out of my pockets. My lungs felt clean, my brain less so, but at least this was an improvement over the emotional whiplash of the morning.

The usual route home took me past two coffee shops, a gym I'd never entered, a boarded-up candy store, and my favorite corner bodega. There was something almost poetic about the consistency of New York bodegas. They all had subtle differences, sure. But no matter the time, weather, or global mood, their neon signs always flickered in the window, and the same sullen old man always seemed to be running the register.

I told myself I'd walk right past, but a sign in the window caught my eye: "HÄAGEN-DAZS 2-FOR-1, ALL FLAVORS." I froze, then backtracked, because sometimes you had to let fate call the shots. I'd been attacked by the memories of my past this morning and now I deserved some sweet, creamy compensation.

Inside, I grabbed two pints of coffee ice cream (the only valid flavor, as far as I was concerned) and cruised through the aisles, just in case there were any new flavors of ramen.

When I stepped up to the counter, the sullen old man gave me his standard look of profound disappointment, then rang up my purchase without a word. I pulled out my credit card, mentally calculated the "I've been good, I deserve this" justification, and tapped.

Declined.

I blinked, then tried again. Still declined.

The sullen old man raised a single world-weary eyebrow. "You got another one?"

I did, but I knew better. The other card was for emergencies only, and if I started treating a Häagen-Dazs craving as an emergency, there was no coming back.

"Uh, hang on," I said, stalling while I fumbled for cash.

I found a five crumpled in my coat pocket, plus some dimes. I slid them across the counter, and the man made no comment, just handed me the bag and muttered, "Receipt?"

"No, thanks." I tucked the ice cream under my arm and hustled outside, cheeks burning in the cold and from embarrassment. Maybe I'd been pushing my luck with the recent takeout splurges, but it wasn't like I'd bought anything extravagant in the past month unless you counted genetic sequencing kits (I'd already maxed out the allowable number specified by my PhD's grant for the fiscal year, sadly) and the commemorative T-shirt from Kaitlyn's baby shower.

Outside, I did what any self-respecting grown woman would do. I sat on a stoop, opened the pint, and began eating the ice cream with the plastic spoon the bodega man had thrown in the bag. I didn't care if it was almost freezing outside. Ice cream, in my opinion, is an anytime food.

It was good, and I hated myself for needing it so badly.

After a few bites, I propped my phone on my knee and logged into my banking app, more out of morbid curiosity than anything else. The interface took an eternity to load, as if it knew what horrors awaited me.

Current balance: $303.46

Next, I checked my credit card. Maxed out, and—oh, great—a missed payment from last month.

I stared at the screen, then at my ice cream, then at the screen again. How had I let this happen? My cheeks burning hotter, I checked my savings account, just to see how close to the red zone I was. As it turns out, I was very close to the red zone. I'd have enough to cover rent and my next student loan payment, maybe, but not if I kept treating ice cream as therapy.

I scooped out another bite, letting the sweet bitterness of the coffee offset my quickly souring mood. If nothing else, the day had at least given me the clarity to see that I needed to change course, stat. No more takeout. No more fancy coffee. No more lunches out with colleagues.

I set the half-eaten pint on the step, wiped my hands on my jeans, and told myself it would be okay. I'd survived worse. I could definitely survive a few weeks or more of extreme austerity.

[5]

PHOTOSYNTHESIS

Samantha

A week of silence and I'd almost convinced myself it had been a hallucination. The bizarre offer, his electric touch, even Andreas's beauty and the way he'd stared at me with those half-lidded olive-green eyes. I'd thrown myself into lab work with the zeal of a person determined to never contemplate babies, or the possibility that one of those babies could be weaponized in a transatlantic corporate pissing match, until I'd finished my PhD.

The problem with this plan was that my department's building was a concrete tomb, it's neoclassical façade an elaborate ruse. The only thing more mind-numbing than running the PCR machine on three hours of sleep was grading undergraduate lab reports for the world's most detail-oriented professor.

Which is where I found myself on a Thursday while trying not to entertain vengeful thoughts. I sat hunched over a battered wooden table in the windowless TA office, red pen poised to massacre the concept of "experimental design" as described by a flock of premeds who'd rather be anywhere but here. If you've never graded a report for a lab course, let me summarize: Never in the history of humanity have so many words been written, so little information conveyed, and so few clues given about what the actual assignment was.

I tried to channel my frustration into productivity. Every time I marked "vague, be specific," I imagined my pen was a tiny sword, stabbing a member of the Kristiansen family (Andreas excluded). I made it through a half stack of blue books—my PI was old-school about lab reports, they all had to be hand-written, likely as a means to combat rampant AI usage—before my phone vibrated, jolting me out of my reverie.

The message was from building security. I squinted at the screen, then at my own handwriting in the margin of the lab report I'd been grading ("Explain how yeast actually works, Kelsey!"), then back at the phone.

"Please come to the lobby. You have a delivery."

I immediately assumed it was Kaitlyn. I'd texted her yesterday to turn down an invitation for dinner and offer to cook for us instead. When she'd pushed the issue, I told her about my vow to go cold turkey on ice cream and takeout, and this had triggered a predictable best friend meltdown in which she tried to Venmo me twice and threatened to order groceries to my door. It would be just like her to send something, possibly a three-tiered Edible Arrangement with "I'm proud of you, Samwise" spelled out in pineapple.

Kaitlyn called me Samwise, as in Samwise Gamgee, her favorite character from Tolkien's epic, *Lord of the Rings*. Strider had been my favorite, predictably. But I didn't mind the nickname because Samwise was a sexy badass and fantastic cook.

Bracing myself for embarrassment and pineapple, I headed down the hallway and toward the elevator, weaving past a pair of lost-looking students who were wearing identical university sweatshirts. The building's lobby was a relic of another era, all faux marble and bulletproof glass. The security desk sat next to a bronze bust of one of the genetics department's founders. Behind the desk, the security guard saw me and nodded toward the waiting area.

"Someone's here for you," he said. "Office is to your left."

I frowned. There was a second glass-enclosed space just off the lobby. I stepped inside, expecting to see a box of fruit.

Instead, standing in front of the window, with the posture of a man who could not believe he'd been made to wait for anything in his entire life, was Tobias Kristiansen.

If Andreas had inherited his mother's Roman goddess genes, Tobias was pure Norse, minus the Viking. He was taller than I remembered, and his suit was navy, tailored to within a micron of his existence. The effect was that of a man who wanted to dominate a boardroom but had never, ever laughed at a fart joke. His blond hair was aggressively parted and his skin was the color of mayonnaise, so pale it practically reflected the fluorescent lights. Despite all this, he was extremely and irritatingly handsome.

I didn't recognize him immediately. It had taken me two point two seconds. This was understandable since I hadn't seen Tobias since my dad's funeral, and even then, he'd stayed on the periphery, too busy being important to make eye contact with a grieving thirteen-year-old. But something in his face was familiar. Maybe it was the nose, objectively small compared to the rest of his features, or the unsettlingly pale blue eyes that tracked me across the room.

"Miss Jarlston," he said, tone modulated for maximum condescension and superiority.

I stopped in the doorway, pulse spiking while my extremities went cold. My first impulse was to turn on my heel and leave. But that would be cowardly, and instinct told me Tobias would almost certainly use it against me later. Instead, I shifted my weight, crossed my arms, and said, "I thought I smelled cabbage."

He smiled, the barest movement of lips. "Thank you for making time for me in your busy, important schedule."

I didn't say anything, because nothing I could say would be as potent as a well-timed silence.

Tobias gestured to the lone chair in the room. "Please, have a seat."

I stood, deliberately.

He shrugged, as if my disobedience was just as he expected. "How is grad school treating you?"

"You don't care, so why ask?"

Another smile, wider this time. "You always were a quick one, Sam."

I hated that he called me Sam. No one called me Sam except for my friends, and he was not in that category.

"How long is this going to take?" I asked, glancing at my phone screen before returning my glare to him. I could've finished grading those reports by now.

He appraised me, gaze moving from my clogs to my scrubs, my lab coat, and the ID badge around my neck, then back to my face. "Direct, smart, and beautiful. I like that. I can see why my little brother is so fixated."

I blanched, my stomach churning. "Excuse me?"

He waved a dismissive hand. "I'll get to the point. You and Andreas, you met."

I thought about denying it, but Andreas had sorta warned me that one of his brothers might contact me. I suspected Tobias kept tabs on Andreas and likely possessed proof that we'd met.

Thus, I shrugged. "So?"

"What did you two discuss?"

"He wanted to catch up," I said, infusing my technically true statement with boredom. "It's been over a decade."

Tobias's eyes narrowed. "You expect me to believe that he just wanted to catch up? Andreas doesn't have friends, Sam. He has adversaries and useful allies. Which are you?"

My jaw clenched. "I don't know what you're talking about."

He stepped closer, and even though there was a desk between us, the sense of threat was real. "See, here's the thing. Genetix is a major donor to your university. In fact, our family's foundation funds a sizable chunk of your department's budget. It would be a shame if something complicated that relationship."

I stared at him, but I plotted an escape route. Security was just outside the door. If I had to run out of here, I'd be fine. "Are you threatening me?"

He shrugged again. "Just letting you know how things work."

"Good. Because here's how they work for me." I put my hands on the back of the plastic chair, gripping it tight enough to make my knuckles go white. "I have no interest in your family—including your little brother—your company, or your money. Andreas sought me out, not the other way around. I told him to get lost. Therefore, I assume we're done."

Tobias administered a slow, appraising look. Then he reached into the inner pocket of his suit and pulled out a slim manila envelope. He set it on the desk with exaggerated care.

"Open it," he said.

I hesitated, then picked it up. Inside were glossy color prints, old-school-private-investigator-style. Obviously, I recognized myself immediately. The photos were in reverse chronological order: me walking out of the café, arms crossed, eyes narrowed; me sitting at a table with Andreas, looking at a piece of paper; me standing on the sidewalk just after Andreas had approached.

I set the photos down, face burning even though Andreas and I hadn't done anything to be embarrassed about. But still. It felt awful to know I'd been spied on and photographed.

"Cute," I said. "I didn't deny we met. What's your point?"

Tobias's voice was patient, almost gentle. "My brother is the best chess player in the world, but otherwise, he's an idiot. He thinks he can get away with . . . whatever this is." He tapped the photos, as if that explained everything. "But you are smarter than that. You know there are consequences to getting involved with my family again. For everyone."

I looked at the photos, then at him. "Why do you care who Andreas speaks to? Don't you have more important things to do than stalk your little brother's social life?"

He bristled. "I am invested in *my* family's company, and in keeping things stable until Father passes. We can't afford distractions."

I shrugged. "Then maybe you should talk to your brother about not ambushing people outside their jobs."

"Or maybe you should stop meeting with him, entertaining his schemes and giving him false hope, or else I will have no choice but to make you suffer," Tobias said, voice dropping to a low whisper.

There was a beat of silence.

I couldn't help it, I started to laugh. Not a big, hearty laugh, but a thin, incredulous one, because of course this family would bully me for absolutely no reason. That was their opening bid, that's all they ever did.

"I see. So, you do know what we discussed. Why pretend otherwise?" I said, going for broke, deciding I'd play around with him, just a little, just enough to irritate the man.

Tobias hesitated, then said, "Why don't you fill me in on what you think I know."

I leaned in, like I was going to spill my darkest secret. "You're right. I was the one to set up the meeting. Because—gosh, I don't know how to say this, and I can't believe you found out so quickly." I pressed my lips together and gave him my best big I'm-so-bashful eyes.

"What? What is it?" he demanded, leaning further over the desk.

"I'm in love with Andreas."

He reared back. "What?"

"I've had a crush on your brother since I was, like, eight. I have a shrine to him in my closet, always have. My prized possession is a paper cup he once used. Sometimes, as night, I press my lips to the rim of the cup and—"

He huffed impatiently, his eyes narrowing.

I wasn't finished. "—pretend we're kissing. So, I finally told him at the coffee shop. Andreas was nice about it and let me down gently. But still, one day, I'm determined that he will be mine."

Tobias looked furious, but also seemed caught off guard, his gaze flicking over me. "I know you are lying."

"How would you know? Did you record our conversation? If you did, you wouldn't be here." Irritating him—even in this small way—felt incredibly satisfying. Better than ten ice-cream pints. This moment and Tobias Kristiansen's frustrated glower would sustain me for months.

"Because Andreas would not have refused your overtures, nor would he have let you down gently." He studied me, suddenly looking tired, lips pressed into a thin line. "Obviously, I do not believe you. You are after something."

I spread my hands. "If I am, it's none of your business. But I suggest you talk to your brother, instead of me."

He glared, then pocketed the envelope. "Stay away from him."

I grinned, because irritating him was the only weapon I had. "Or what? You'll have me kicked out of grad school? Remove funding for the college? Have your goons follow me to my favorite bagel shop and buy out all the chive cream cheese before I can order?"

He shook his head, eyes skating over me, seeming genuinely perplexed. "I understand his preoccupation, now that I have seen you again. But you are more trouble than you are worth, Sam."

"Right back at you, *Toby*."

Tobias opened his mouth, likely to object to my usage of his child-hood moniker, but just then, my phone buzzed again. I looked down, expecting another passive-aggressive message from Kaitlyn about accepting her food offerings, but it was from Dmitry.

Dmitry: Your plates are done. What do you want me to do with the samples? Also, Dr. Nieminen says hi.

I smiled grimly, then looked up at Tobias, who was still standing there, radiating contempt but also curiosity. The curiosity felt more dangerous.

"Sorry, gotta run," I said, lifting my phone. "Duty calls."

He straightened to his full height again, but not before muttering, "You would do well to remember my warning."

"You sound like a Disney villain. Get a better writer," I shot back, already halfway out the door.

I headed for the elevator, adrenaline pounding in my ears, and hit the up button twice just for the satisfaction of it. As the doors closed behind me, I replayed the entire encounter, and three statements stood out as particularly alarming.

I can see why my little brother is so fixated.

Because Andreas would not have refused your overtures, nor would he have let you down gently.

I understand his preoccupation.

"Damn it," I muttered, giving my head a shake and resolving to ignore Tobias's statements.

Tobias Kristiansen was just as diabolical as his father. Maybe he'd said those things to unsettle me and get under my skin. Or maybe they served some other evil, strategic purpose. Nothing that man said should be accepted as truth, I knew that. The only thing I could do was get on with my life.

Let go of the past. Let it all go.

Forget Tobias. Forget that psycho family.

But Andreas isn't a psycho.

My steps slowed and I felt my frown intensify as the image of adult Andreas sitting across from me in that café last week replayed again in my mind for the millionth time in seven days. I tried closing my eyes, but it was no use. He was still there, reaching across the table, staring at me, voice gentle.

Ugh. This is the worst.

Thank goodness I still had the other pint of ice cream in my freezer at home. I was going to need it.

[6]
CELLULAR RESPIRATION

Samantha

After the day I'd had—after Tobias and his glossy photos, the threat to my academic future, and the three-hour marathon of grading half-literate premed lab reports—I was so tired that the edges of the world looked sanded down.

Yet, I couldn't sleep. This was not unusual for me, but sleep had been markedly elusive for the last week. I simply lay there, arms at my sides, staring at the water stains above my bed, and tried not to think about Tobias's threats. And Andreas. Again.

And if I somehow succeeded at pushing thoughts of the Kristiansens from my mind, my dumb brain would then remind me that my grandma's savings account, the one I'd promised myself I would only ever touch in a real emergency, was now $708.63 lighter than it had been twelve hours ago.

Even with my Teaching Assistantship and work-study paycheck, even with the elaborate system of ramen rotation and energy-bar rationing, grad school in Manhattan was like feeding hundred-dollar bills into a paper shredder. The rent had cleared today, as it did every month, and I'd felt the click of it in my chest.

Grandma's money wasn't anywhere close to gone, but I hated using it. When I closed my eyes, I could see her writing a check in perfect, old-lady cursive, with tidy, sweeping loops. I never cashed her checks when she was alive, but in her will she'd left all her savings to me, making me promise, on her actual deathbed, not to use the money for "anything stupid or self-destructive, like revenge."

I could take out more student loans, but I really, really, really didn't want to. I already had to pay back my law school loans. Becoming and being a PhD geneticist was a labor of love; no one in theoretical science and bench research was here for fame, fortune, or glory.

Maybe I should've just practiced law for a few years first, paid back the loans, made bank, and then returned to school. Too late now.

Shaking my head, I tried closing my eyes again. Somewhere in the apartment, a radiator shuddered, then spat out a series of hollow clanks that perfectly echoed the arrhythmia of my thoughts. I reached for my phone; the screen told me it was now just past 1:00 AM; I'd lain down at 10:30 PM. There were no new texts. I checked my email. A single line from my PI sent ten minutes ago: "Can you meet tomorrow at 11 to discuss sequencing results?" I marked it unread, like that would somehow keep the obligation at bay. But I'd be there, if only I could get some sleep.

Rolling onto my side, I stared at the prescription bottle on my nightstand. The sleeping pills were supposed to be for emergencies only, which my therapist had described as when my brain was actively hostile. I'd made it almost to Thanksgiving this year, seven months since I'd last taken one, which was a new record. But as the minutes slid by and my brain kept insisting I think about Andreas and money and my grandmother, I decided this insistence counted as hostility.

I popped the cap off the sleeping pills, shook one into my palm, and swallowed it dry. The bitterness spread across my tongue, a microsecond of revolt, and then nothing. Just the promise of oblivion.

To maximize my odds of making it to campus on time for the 11:00 AM meeting with my PI, I set three alarms—9:30, 10:00, and 10:30— in case the first two failed to breach the drug fog. I double-checked that

I'd plugged in my phone. My sleep hygiene was a disaster, but at least my alarm game was strong.

I burrowed back under the covers and did the thing my therapist called "progressive relaxation." First, the toes. Then the calves. Then the quads. It was supposed to work like hypnosis, but mostly it made me hyper-aware that I hadn't shaved my legs in four weeks, and that my calves were now 80 percent tension, 20 percent bone.

Somewhere in the process, the pill hit. Not like a sledgehammer. More like the slow and quiet dying of a fire. The next thing I knew, I was in a dream.

It was a room that could have been any room, but the walls pulsed with a kind of warm glow, like I viewed it through stained glass. Sun through dust motes, the hum of an ancient fan, the thump of tennis shoes on hardwood. I was twelve, I knew that for sure, because I could see my own knees, sharp and unscarred, poking out from a pair of cutoff shorts that used to be my favorite.

Andreas was there. Not the current, Roman statue version, but the kid I remembered. Eleven years old, hair a dark riot, eyes enormous, always on the edge of either tears or laughter. He was stacking pillows on the floor with a focus so intense it looked like he was planning the Normandy invasion. A pillow fort. When he noticed me, he grinned, wide and guileless.

He said something, voice insistent, but the words were garbled.

I responded, and I could hear my own kid-voice, awkward and crackly, but again the words didn't make sense.

The pillows rearranged themselves until the structure wasn't just a fort; it was a labyrinth. We built it higher and wider than any pillow and blanket fort had a right to be, stealing every pillow, every chair, every bit of fabric. There was a sense of real urgency, like the whole world depended on our ability to barricade ourselves in.

At some point, the walls started to change. The colors got brighter, the edges sharper. Suddenly I was myself again, or at least the version of myself that existed now. Twenty-eight, five foot eight, long limbs, pale skin. Andreas was also older, though I hadn't seen it happen. One minute he was a kid, the next he was a giant in the six-thousand-dollar coat, arms longer and stronger, eyes the same improbable shade of green.

We were sitting inside the blanket fort, knees almost touching, and I could feel my face get hot with the knowledge of him. The knowledge that we'd once been children together, and now we were not.

He reached out, one big, careful hand, and cupped my cheek. His fingers were cool and dry, but his thumb was gentle as he brushed it along my jawline.

"I want to marry you," he said, voice echoing. It was what he'd said in the café, but this time the words were softer, like an apology or an incantation.

"Why?" dream-me asked, hoping for something I couldn't name.

"You deserve revenge," he said, his tone sounding like an out-of-tune piano. Or perhaps it was the words. All I knew was, he'd given me the wrong answer. This wasn't right. This wasn't how we were supposed to meet each other or be together.

I tried to pull away, but his grip was both light and inescapable.

"You don't want me. You just want to use me," I whispered.

His eyes were so open it hurt to look at them. "We will use each other."

I shook my head. This man wasn't Andreas. Andreas would never suggest something like this. He wasn't that kind of person.

I tried to move, tried to push myself backward through the pillow wall, but the fort had become a maze, and every time I thought I'd found the exit, he was already there, waiting for me with those hands and those eyes and his sad, perfect patience.

"Let me go," I pleaded.

He shook his head, slow and almost fondly. "I won't."

My hands were fists, my fingers fused together as one, and I couldn't look at him. "But you did."

He reached out again, fingers spreading, and he said, "Sam!" but his voice was wrong.

I opened my mouth to yell for help and he disappeared.

"Sam?"

I awoke to the sound of someone clapping. I stood in the middle of the kitchen, barefoot, one arm clutching my pillow like a flotation device. My hair was a nest, some of it in my face.

Diya hovered by the stove, her eyes wide and her lips parted.

"You okay?" Her tone sounded oddly soft and so totally at odds with the chaos of my dream that it made me want to burst into tears.

I looked around, tried to orient myself. The clock on the microwave read 5:06 AM. The only light was the under-cabinet LED.

"I—" My throat was dry. "How did I get here?"

Diya moved a step closer. "I was following you to make sure you didn't walk out the door. You went into the living room, then back to our room, then back here."

I sank to the floor, knees up, pillow still clutched tight. "Sorry. Sorry. I don't usually—that doesn't happen anymore." I wasn't awake yet, not fully. Between the dream and the sleeping pills, my brain felt impossibly foggy.

She sat down opposite me on the kitchen floor, cross-legged and wearing her favorite pair of tie-dyed pajama pants. "You were sleep-walking."

I repeated, "Sleepwalking."

"Have you ever done this before?"

Pushing my hair out of my face, I nodded. "I used to when I was a teenager, after my parents . . ." *After my parents died.*

Diya knew my parents had passed away before I turned eighteen, but that was all she knew. I wasn't a big fan of talking about my past. Better to focus on the present and future than dwell unnecessarily on old, unchangeable events.

I felt her study me for a long moment, then she asked, "Has something stressful happened recently?"

"No," I lied, staring at my bare feet. "Just the usual." I glanced at her.

She watched me, a doctor's gaze, patient but also methodical. "You know, sometimes these things start up again when there's a trigger. Even a small one."

"Yeah," I said, voice barely more than a whisper. "Makes sense."

Diya was silent for a bit, then leaned over and gently pried the pillow from my grip. "You ever try talking about it?"

"About what?"

She gave me a look like, *Seriously, dude?* "Whatever is making you sleepwalk through the apartment tonight."

I shook my head. "It's nothing. Just dreams."

"Bad dreams?"

I shrugged. "Not really. Just . . . weird. Nostalgic, I guess."

There was a pause, and then Diya handed my pillow back. "If you need to talk, just let me know."

"Noted." I hugged the pillow to my chest again, trying to will my heartbeat into something resembling normal.

Diya started to say something else, but then stopped herself. Instead, she stood, stretched, and flicked the light off.

"Good night, Sam," she said, and padded back to our room.

I stayed on the floor a few minutes longer, just breathing and trying not to cry. Eventually, I shuffled back to my own bed, still clutching the pillow, and lay there in the darkness, counting watermarks and waiting for the silence to take shape again.

* * *

I awoke with the 9:30 AM alarm and to the distant, muffled sound of my roommates' voices. The memory of my sleepwalking episode from last night kept me in bed even though I had to pee like a racehorse. Eventually, I flipped back the covers and ran to the bathroom, hoping I wouldn't have to stand outside the door doing the pee-pee dance for very long.

The fates favored me because the bathroom was empty. But after completing my business and as I washed my hands, I caught sight of my hair in the mirror over the sink. Sleep-matted and greasy at the roots, it was approaching "self-aware ecosystem" status.

When was the last time I showered? One of life's unanswerable questions.

Yanking my hair back in a high ponytail, I washed my face and brushed my teeth. Then, feeling moderately more human, I stumbled into the hallway. Blinking at the too-bright world, I stretched as I walked into the little kitchen, Diya's and Nakita's low, conspiratorial whispers ending abruptly at my entrance. They were both sitting at the tiny two-person rectangular table that doubled as extra counter space.

"Morning," I croaked, voice two registers below normal as I shuffled past.

Diya looked up from her mug, eyes doing a quick scan of my form. "Hey. You slept in."

Nakita, by contrast, didn't bother with the subtlety. "Why are you sleepwalking? Diya said you used to when you were a kid? Why? Because of your parents? Did something happen?"

I glanced at Diya. She'd lowered her forehead to her palm, her face turned to the side toward Nakita, presumably to give our roommate an intense stink eye while mouthing, *Shut up!*

And this, ladies and gentlemen, was one of the reasons why I didn't talk about myself, or my past, to anyone.

While wracking my fuzzy brain for a deflecting joke, I poured a glass of water and sipped it. "I sleepwalk when a storm's a comin'. Some people have knees that hurt when it rains, I sleepwalk."

Diya exchanged a look with Nakita. There was a silent communication there, a kind of backchannel that only develops between people who gossip both before and after breakfast.

"So," Diya said, "any plans for today?"

"Meeting with my PI at eleven. Then lab stuff," I said. "Might grade some reports. Why?"

She hesitated, then asked, "Do you have any days off planned? Maybe a weekend at your friend Kaitlyn's mansion in the Hamptons?"

Kaitlyn had invited me to her family's place in the Hamptons, right on the beach, it was true. But the house was a two-bedroom cottage, not a mansion. It had belonged to Kaitlyn's grandmother, who'd been a physicist in the 1930s and '40s. Kaitlyn's family tree was like a who's who for notable US scientists and politicians.

"Yeah," Nakita chimed in. "You should take some time off, you seem stressed."

I put my hand over my mouth and yawned, hard, then leaned against the wall for support. "Yeah, okay. I'll think about it. Are there any of my eggs left in the fridge?"

Diya set down her mug, her expression gentle. "You know, sleep-walking is super rare in adults. Like, one or two in a hundred."

"Guess I'm special." I tried to smile, frustrated that my roommates wouldn't take a hint and drop the subject.

Diya opened her mouth again, likely to press me further, but the apartment buzzer went off, sounding like an electrified goose. All three of us jumped.

"And now I'm fully awake." My hand flew to my heart and I closed my eyes, laughing.

Nakita, closest to the entry, stood. "I'll get it," she said, and vanished around the corner.

I bent and peered into the fridge, spotting two hard-boiled eggs in a glass dish. "Can I eat these?" I lifted the dish and gave it a little shake.

"Go ahead, I boiled them this morning." Diya took a sip from her mug, watching me over the rim.

In the background, I heard Nakita at the intercom. "Who is it?"

A voice crackled back, slightly distorted but still perfectly recognizable. "Andreas Kristiansen, here to see Samantha."

[7]

DNA, RNA, AND PROTEINS

Samantha

For a moment, the world went completely silent except for the slow metronome of my heart in my ears. There was no way it was him. Couldn't be. No way he'd show up at my apartment.

And yet, I'd heard his voice crackling through the old door speaker, *Andreas Kristiansen, here to see Samantha.*

Diya's eyes cut to mine, then away, then back again, a question behind them. Unable to spare a single synapse to regulate my facial expression, I simply stared at her in return, straining my ears.

Nakita, never one for subtlety, snorted. "Yeah, right. Get lost."

There was a beat of dead air, and then through the intercom, "Please tell Samantha that Andreas is here for her." He sounded irritated.

All at once, I was out of the kitchen, sprinting to the wall-mounted speaker. I pressed the button with a trembling thumb. "I'm here. Sorry. Andreas, I'm buzzing you in."

The response was a flat, "Thank you," with an intonation that made it sound suspiciously like, *Finally.*

Then *click.* Silence.

When I turned around, both Diya and Nakita were staring at me with curiosity, but Nakita's eyes also held disbelief. "Wait. You actually know someone named Andreas Kristiansen?"

I bit my lip. "Yeah. He's—" I tried to figure out how to explain him without triggering an avalanche of follow-up questions. "We go way back."

Diya, master of the understated eyebrow, let hers inch upward. "Should I recognize the name? And, by 'way back,' do you mean to the childhood you never talk about?"

I tried to smile and huff out a laugh. It came out more like a snort. "Yes. Childhood. Our parents were—uh—business partners." This was the biggest understatement since "the Titanic ran into a little trouble."

Nakita's brain appeared to be working at double speed now. "But—like—is it *that* Andreas Kristiansen?"

I played dumb and tried employing a non sequitur, which sometimes distracted her enough for me to plot an escape. "He's not a politician, if that's what you mean."

"Who is Andreas Kristiansen?" Diya glanced between Nakita and me.

Nakita shook her head vigorously, ponytail whipping, ignoring Diya. She reached out and gripped my upper arm. "No, no, I mean the chess guy. The prodigy? Best player in the world? The dude who destroys other grand masters in thirty seconds or less and then just walks off stage like, whatever. That's your Andreas?"

I tried not to grimace and failed. "I don't know. Who's to say. It's been a while since we—" The sound of heavy footsteps on the stairs cut me off.

The color drained from Nakita's face. "Holy shit. It's him, right? Is he coming up? Oh my God. You know Andreas Kristiansen! Why didn't you say anything? I would've put on pants!"

I wiped my palms down my thighs, a new burst of adrenaline making my hands sweat. "It's not a big deal. He's just a person. Also, you're literally wearing pants."

"I meant real pants, not pajama pants!" she hissed.

There was a knock on the door and all three of us flinched like house cats sprayed with water.

Diya, the only person in the apartment who could reliably do anything with grace, peered out the peephole and then looked back at me, her eyes three sizes bigger than normal. "You should get the door," she whispered, then to Nakita added, "Are all chess players so hot? Holy shit!"

I hesitated, then motioned for Nakita to stand to my left. "Back up," I whispered. Nakita nodded gravely, like this was the most important moment of her life.

With my heart banging against my ribs, I undid the chain and the three dead bolts, then turned the knob and swung the door open.

There he was, brooding in a black wool coat and a perfectly ironed dark green button-up, standing in my doorway, looking as though he'd just stepped out of a magazine cover. His hair was a little messier than last week, and his dark, thick eyebrows were drawn low over those absurdly intense eyes. He looked annoyed, but also a bit wary.

"Hello, Samantha," he said, voice low and—God help me—still unreasonably attractive.

I realized I was just standing there, holding the doorknob with both hands like an idiot. "Uh. Hi. Come in."

He did, brushing past me in a wave of cool air and rosemary-scented something, pausing at the entryway table. He sized up Diya and Nakita, then looked back at me as if waiting for an introduction.

Nakita, apparently unable to contain herself, blurted, "Oh my God, you're Andreas Kristiansen!"

His face did not move. "Yes."

I turned to Nakita and shot her the most vicious side-eye I could muster. "Can you not?"

She grinned, hands clasped under her chin now. "Sorry, but do you even know how much I am freaking out right now? My sister would lose her mind if she knew you were in our apartment. She literally talks about you every day. Like, every day."

Andreas looked at me, then at her. "Your sister plays chess?"

Nakita nodded. "She plays tournaments, women's chess."

This was news to me, but it tracked with everything I knew about Nakita's family.

Diya interjected, "What's 'women's chess'? Why isn't it just chess?"

Andreas held his gloved fingers out to Diya for a shake. "Andreas."

"Diya," she said, accepting the handshake.

"The short answer is, women's chess exists because men are horrible," Andreas answered her question, very matter-of-factly. "But it persists because not many girls and women play chess—for many reasons—and therefore women make more money in women's chess."

Diya made a choking sound, her eyes widening with surprise, presumably at his candor.

But Nakita only grinned wider. "My sister has a livestream account with a ton of followers. She sits in Central Park and challenges people to games in real time. If they win, she pays them fifty dollars."

"Does she ever have to pay out?" Diya asked.

"No, never." Nakita beamed. "But a lot of men get angry—I mean, absolutely furious—when they lose."

I was trying to keep up and abruptly realized the door was still open. I shut it and took the opportunity to shake out my hands, telling myself I had no reason to be so nervous.

"Ah, yes. I think I've seen her videos." Andreas nodded subtly. "She has a strong end game, but favors the Ruy Lopez."

Nakita gasped and inched forward like she might grab him. "Are you serious? We are such huge fans. She would absolutely die if she could play you. Or just meet you."

Andreas's expression remained unreadable, but he sounded thoughtful as he said, "I do not usually play strangers in parks."

Diya, who'd watched the interaction between Nakita and Andreas like a true spectator, gave him the once-over. "Do you play women?"

"Whenever my counterparts are willing, of course. But I am a man and therefore not allowed to play in women's chess tournaments."

Diya crossed her arms. "And do you always win when you play women?"

He stared at her for a beat, then said, "I generally win, no matter who I play."

I couldn't decide if he sounded arrogant or not, so I looked at Nakita to see if his words bothered her. She was still grinning at him like he'd invented cheese. Either she didn't notice his arrogance or wasn't bothered by it.

"But, yes. I have lost to a player before who happened to be a woman." Andreas, tone flat, began removing his gloves.

My heart spiked, pulse fluttering, and I grabbed his wrist to still his movements before he could reveal his ridiculously sexy hands. "Are you here to—why are you here? I mean, what do you want?"

"I want to talk to you," he said, voice low, communicating with a small incline of his head that he'd prefer to speak in private. Which, given the crowd, was fair.

And, just in case I hadn't understood his head tilt, he added, "Alone, if possible." His voice was a touch softer than before.

I glanced around the crowded entryway and then toward the small sitting area and even smaller kitchen. "Sure, we can . . ." I trailed off, searching for a more private venue than the kitchen table.

Diya saved me, gesturing down the hall. "Use our room," she said, the faintest smile ghosting her lips. "I'll keep Nakita occupied. Come on, Nakita, let's go see if my chai chia pudding recipe actually worked."

Nakita frowned for the first time since Andreas had walked in, shooting me a look that threatened, *We'll talk later!* and followed Diya toward the kitchen, her head turning back toward us with every few steps.

Andreas waited until they'd disappeared before facing me. "Lead the way."

And, with my heart in my throat, I did.

I realized as we walked down the hallway that I'd left a week's worth of dirty laundry in a mountainous heap in the middle of the floor last night, sorted and ready for the coin laundry down the street. I also realized that my desk probably looked like a tornado had passed through, if that tornado had a fondness for empty ramen bowls, highlighters, and sticky notes with things like "NIEMINEN IS A GNOME WITH TINY HANDS" written in all caps.

Preemptively mortified, I hurried ahead and started scooping up clothes, balling them into a nest and shoving them into my closet, which immediately caused a small avalanche of more items to tumble out.

Andreas watched the process in silence, hands still gloved and hanging at his sides. He looked slightly less out of place in my tiny room than he had in the entryway, but only slightly.

"You share this room," he observed.

Finally able to shut the closet door by pressing my back against it, I pointed at the cracked faux-leather desk chair. "You can sit. Sorry about . . . all of this." I waved my hand, taking in the entirety of my mess.

He walked to the chair, sat, then tugged at the leather around his wrists and at his fingertips. I tried not to watch, but it felt impossible. Cheeks flushing, I turned my back until I could be sure his gloves were off. Pretending to straighten my nightstand became clearing off my nightstand as I swiped the contents—including the sleeping pills but not the lamp—into the top drawer.

Crossing my arms, I twisted at the waist just in time to see him tuck his gloves into his coat pocket. Andreas then set his elbows on the chair arms. He may have appeared bored to someone who didn't grow up with him, but I recognized the calculating quality behind those droopy-lidded eyes.

"You have more roommates?" he asked, glancing at the closed door behind me.

"Three in total," I replied as I gathered a pile of textbooks from the floor at the foot of my bed and stacked them on the windowsill. "Diya and Nakita, both of whom you just met briefly, plus Kendra. I could've signed up for subsidized housing through the University, but this place is actually less expensive."

He frowned, as if I'd confessed to sleeping in a dumpster. "You feel safe? To share a room?"

I stared at him and his question, at a loss.

His face reassembled itself into something perfectly neutral, but he added, "You might recall, my brother Henrik and I shared a room, for a time."

"Ah, yes." Now his question made sense. "I remember. And, yes. Diya is great. I trust her."

Andreas's stare seemed to drill into mine, as though hoping to pull the truth out of me with the force of his attention alone. When I said nothing else, he glanced away, dusting the fabric of his black pants with the back of his fine fingers.

"So . . ." I glanced behind me to ensure I wouldn't be sitting on another pile of laundry; finding the space empty save for the mattress and covers, I sat on my bed. "What brings you to my humble abode?"

Andreas exhaled, the sound almost imperceptible, but enough for me to know he was still irritated. "I wanted to talk."

"We're talking now."

His eyes seemed to darken. "You didn't call."

I blinked. "When?"

The subtle shift in the line of his mouth told me he was already losing patience. "After Tobias visited you yesterday. I requested that you let me know if he or Henrik bothered you."

Oh. That.

I crossed my arms again, fighting against a strange sense of disappointment, and I felt my own temper begin to simmer. "I never agreed to your request."

"It would be wise to keep me apprised." His voice was ice-water calm, which only made his words sound condescending.

I didn't respond. Not for the first time this week, I reminded myself that we weren't anything to each other. I owed him nothing, not even an explanation. *And he owes me nothing.*

Andreas leaned back in the desk chair, studying me with a flat, cold intensity that reminded me of a microscope. "He will escalate. You know that, right?"

"If he does, I'll deal with it." I couldn't explain it, not even to myself, but I didn't want Andreas to be here because of Tobias, or Genetix, or any reason related to his family or mine. And the fact that *this*—Tobias's unwelcomed visit yesterday—was the purpose of Andreas's visit today, annoyed me.

He tapped his fingers on the arms of the chair, his gaze assessing, evaluating, calculating. "You should have called me."

I looked at the water stains on the ceiling, then at the closet door where I'd just shoved my laundry, then at him. "This is getting us nowhere. What exactly do you want, Andreas?"

He was silent for a long moment, his eyes flicking over my face, my arms, my posture, as if recalibrating some internal schema. Finally, he said, "I want to protect you."

Something about the way he said it made my pulse trip. Not in a romantic way. More like how you feel when a fire alarm goes off in the middle of an exam and you don't know if it's a drill or the real thing.

"Don't," I said, more softly than I meant. "If that's why you're here, you should leave."

Andreas's jaw flexed. "You should not have to deal with Tobias and his threats. I know he threatened you. I know—"

"If you felt that way, then you should've left me alone," I snapped, the words out before I could choke them back. "You're the reason I'm on his radar now."

Eyes narrowed, exhaling through his nose, he stood abruptly. The chair nearly toppled over, but he caught it, steadied it, and then turned to face me. "If you had answered my messages last month, all of this could have been avoided."

"If you'd left well enough alone, then Tobias wouldn't have shown up yesterday." I also stood, squaring my shoulders, not caring how angry I sounded. "Why would I trust you to protect me from a situation you created?"

Something like fury passed behind his features. "You really want Henrik or Tobias to inherit your father's company? Is that what you want?"

I said nothing, clenching my hands until my knuckles hurt. I couldn't bring myself to lie about this again like I'd done in the coffee shop, especially not after seeing Tobias yesterday.

"Answer me," he demanded.

"No," I whisper-shouted, having just enough wherewithal to keep my voice down so as not to give Nakita and Diya something new to gossip about. "No, I don't. I want revenge. I want them destitute and desperate. I want the company so badly, I can't sleep at night thinking about your evil father and all the ways I wish he would suffer. I hope your entire family—you excluded—dies in a fire. Happy?"

He didn't reply. Instead, he took a step back, his chin lifting as he stared at me and my ugly confessions.

I realized I'd gone too far, but the anger wouldn't stop choking me. I wanted to be finished with my past bitterness and resentment, but my true feelings had spiraled out, vengefulness saturating my words. I dropped my eyes and stared at the threadbare carpet, wishing I could go back to the version of myself that existed before my admission ten seconds ago, before seeing him last week, before all of it.

Why did he come here? Why can't he just leave me alone?

My heart ached, just like last week. And the rubber bands around my lungs returned, squeezing tight.

Rubbing my forehead, I heaved a sigh and it was just on the tip of my tongue to ask him to leave when he said, "I'm not only here because of Tobias."

I blinked, peeking at him, unsure what to do with that. "Oh?"

He hesitated, then moved closer. Not in a threatening way, just enough to bridge the gap between us. "I have found another way to ensure you inherit Genetix upon my father's death. And do not worry, it does not involve anything you might find revolting, like marrying me or having my child." For once, he'd allowed emotion to enter his voice, and it sounded like disdain.

I bit back a sarcastic response, instead grinding out, "Fine. What is it?"

He hesitated for a split second, then said, "I will adopt you."

I stared at him, waiting for him to say, *Just kidding*, or, *Got you!*

When he didn't, I blinked. Then blinked again. His passive stare— deadly serious, not even a hint of humor in it—told me what I could not accept from his words alone. I realized he meant it.

He meant it. *He's serious.*

"You have read the pertinent page of the will, it makes no mention of marriage or any other type of union, nor does it state that the grand-child needs to be biological." Andreas sounded as though he were explaining the rules to a card game and not outlining why it made sense for him to *adopt* me. "It merely states 'first grandchild.' When I adopt you, you will obviously be the first. You're two years older than me, which—given the situation—is somewhat amusing."

I stared at him, completely dumbstruck, my brain floundering. "But —but—"

I searched for the flaw, the trick, the punchline, and found none.

The side of his mouth hitched but his gaze was wholly and starkly devoid of humor as he asked, "So, what say you, Samantha? Will you consent to be my daughter?"

[8]

GENES AND HEREDITY

Samantha

The city felt several degrees colder than the week before, and I ducked my nose inside my thick scarf as I scuttled east on Seventy-Third, hands deep in my coat pockets and chin tucked low. A fierce wind funneled straight down the cross streets, whipping at my hair and occasionally flinging it across my face like I'd pissed off some minor weather deity.

It was seven o'clock in the evening, give or take a minute, and the sky was that weird color it gets just after dark in early winter, less blue, more like a violet bruise above the city skyline. Every inhale had that metallic cold-snap taste and my breath became clouds of white with every exhale.

I passed a mother in a Canada Goose parka dragging her son by the wrist while he mewled about not wanting to go to flute lessons. The doorman in front of Kaitlyn's building smiled at me, an avuncular twitch of the mouth that said, *You don't live here, but I recognize you.* I smiled back. He reminded me of my grandpa, and I briefly considered calling him.

But, no. My grandfather and I hadn't talked since he'd remarried and moved to Arizona.

Kaitlyn's apartment building was the kind of structure you saw in movies about people who never worried about health insurance or whether one ramen serving could be stretched into two full meals with enough broccoli. The lobby was marble, the elevator was wood-paneled, and the whole place had that subtle, permanent scent of new carpet mixed with whatever they used to clean glass.

If you let Andreas adopt you and you inherit Genetix, then you'd be able to afford an apartment in a building with a doorman, no problem. Maybe even the whole damn building.

I sighed.

As the elevator ferried me up, I tried, for maybe the thousandth time, to make a decision about Andreas's offer. It had been just two days, but it had felt like weeks since he'd stood in my tiny apartment and explained his plan.

Andreas, even as a child, had been the type to make amends for the sake of his own internal sense of righteousness. More and more, I was beginning to suspect that he'd only reached out to me in an attempt to correct a wrong between our respective families, settle a debt, make things right.

But for me . . . my intentions and motivations for considering his offer were much less virtuous.

Also, both my past and current feelings for Andreas Kristiansen didn't have much to do with correcting historical injustices. Mind you, none of my present feelings for (i.e., attraction to) Andreas were at all voluntary. A fact that didn't stop the attraction from existing. Even sleep-deprived, even discombobulated and emotional and blindsided, both times he'd popped up unannounced, I couldn't seem to stop checking him out.

How incredibly inconvenient.

But here's the thing about attraction: It always fades.

See, attraction is like a plant. If you water it too much, it dies. If you water it too little, it also dies. And that's the key to killing attraction. Over time, with either enough exposure or enough distance, it goes away. Thus, either I needed A LOT more exposure to Andreas—like, daily—or I needed to cut him out of my life.

I was currently leaning toward cutting him out. True, I'd asked Andreas for time to think about his plan. In reality, I hadn't stopped thinking about it for even a second.

I also hadn't told anyone. Not my therapist, not Diya, obviously not my grandfather, not even Kaitlyn. Which was why I was here now, in front of her apartment, steeling myself before the door.

I pressed the little call button and waited.

"Sam!" Kaitlyn's excited voice sounded from the speaker. They had an app on their phones, instead of a built-in intercom, that allowed them to interact with door-button pushers.

Despite my mood, I tried to sound chipper. "Hey, it's me."

The lock buzzed. I entered and let myself in to the warmth and soft golden light of the apartment. I used to love coming here just after Kaitlyn and Martin got married. The apartment belonged to them both, but the grand piano was entirely Kaitlyn's. She'd changed her major in college to music theory and now did what she loved, writing compositions for famous singers and collaborating with famous songwriters.

Kaitlyn's family had money, but not a Standard-Oil-before-the-trust-breakup amount. Her mother was a senator and her father was the dean of the School of Medicine at UCLA. So, well-off, but not tech-bro well-off. Martin's father was the absurdly wealthy one in their family tree, but both Martin and Kaitlyn had severed ties with the telecom giant years ago.

Still, every square foot of the apartment screamed antique and quality, and nothing looked cheap or temporary.

I hung my coat on the rack by the door, then called out, "Where are you?"

From somewhere deeper in the apartment, her voice called back, "Come in! I'm at the piano."

I padded down the hallway, past the powder room and the minimalist kitchen, and into the living room, where Kaitlyn sat perched on the piano bench with a mug in one hand and a pencil in the other. She seemed to be writing something in an open notebook set on the music stand. Her curly, dark brown hair was up in a bun and tonight she wore black leggings, a wildly oversized red turtleneck, and not a stitch of makeup.

She stood as I entered and set her mug down on the mission-style coffee table.

"Sam," she said, and her face lit up with real joy, her big smile showing off the subtle gap between her two front teeth. She never used my full name, unless it was in print or on a birthday cake. "Get over here, you gorgeous beast."

We hugged. She always went for a full-body embrace, even if one of us was holding something sharp or breakable. There was a long moment of pure, unspoken comfort. I tried to remember the last time I'd hugged anyone longer than five seconds.

It was the last time you saw Kaitlyn.

"Where's the baby?" I asked, pulling away.

"Martin is in the nursery rocking him. If he's still awake, you can go peek in before you leave, but he's been a monster all day and the last thing anyone needs is him catching a second wind." Kaitlyn grinned. "Sorry if I stink, I'm in feral momma mode and I have a deadline on this new song with Abram."

I looked her up and down, then gestured at myself: scrubby jeans, fraying cardigan, T-shirt I'd found at the bottom of my laundry. "If this is feral, I'm basically a trash panda in human skin."

She grinned, reaching for her mug again. "You say that, but you have no idea what feral is until the aroma of sour breast milk seasons all your clothes. Here, sit, I have a new tea I want you to try."

Kaitlyn motioned me toward the sofa, then disappeared into the kitchen to retrieve the tea. I glanced at the piano and noticed the book she'd placed on the bench—*The Queen's Gambit*.

Not subtle.

Last night, when I'd called to see if she had time for me to come over, I hadn't told her about Andreas's offers to marry me / impregnant me / adopt me, but I had told her that my old friend Andreas Kristiansen had reached out with a proposition, and I wanted to discuss it with her. Kaitlyn, being a nerd, already knew who he was in the chess world. She also already knew a bit about my history with him. I'd shared more of myself and my past with Kaitlyn than I had with any other (non-therapist) person in my life.

She returned with a new mug, handed it to me, and plopped onto the large leather couch, tucking her feet under her. "Tell me everything."

I took a sip. It tasted faintly of cardamom and something sweet. "Oh! It's good."

"I think so. That's fenugreek that you're tasting. It increases breast milk production."

I froze, cup halfway to my mouth.

She laughed. "It won't do anything to nonlactating humans, you goose."

Regardless, I set the mug on the coffee table and folded my hands.

"Okay, now tell me, what's going on with your old friend Andreas? What's this proposition? This is the youngest in that family that screwed over your family, right?"

I inhaled, exhaled, and prepared to sound ridiculous. "Yes, the Kristiansens are the family in question. And yes, the father—his name is Oskar—and potentially the oldest son—let's call him Satan, even though his Christian name is Tobias—framed my father for fraud."

I then went on to summarize how my father, while under an active criminal investigation, lost his shares in his own company, was voted out by the board, declared bankruptcy, and then died of a sudden and massive heart attack.

Kaitlyn listened patiently to the CliffsNotes version of a story she'd heard before, her features soft with compassion. "So, we hate everyone in this family but the youngest, Andreas. And wasn't teenage you in love with him? Or am I thinking of someone else?"

I felt my face heat up. "Not in love. More like . . . I don't know how to describe it." *Crap.*

This sometimes happened when I spoke to Kaitlyn or my therapist. They'd make an offhanded comment, or an assumption, and then things about myself—my past behavior and my past choices—would suddenly make sense.

The reason you can't stop thinking about Andreas and the reason why your body goes haywire whenever you see him now is probably because you had a serious crush on him back then, dummy.

"Okay, sure. He was something like my first love, but I was only thirteen, and he was eleven, so it doesn't count. We were too young for those kinds of feelings, or at least he was. In any case, it was one-sided."

Her eyes narrowed. "Sam. That would make him your *only* love."

"Whatever." I needed to stop explaining about the past since, back then, I hadn't been certain what I'd felt. They'd been emotions I didn't possess any context for at the time as an extremely sheltered thirteen-year-old. And did it matter? I'd been a kid. He'd been a kid. Kid-feelings fifteen years ago shouldn't matter to grown adults.

I pressed on. "Anyway, last week—"

"Wait." She reached forward. "Do you still have feelings for him?"

I flinched back. "What? No! Like I said, we were kids."

Her eyes narrowed and skated over me. "Are you sure? What did you feel when he contacted you?"

I rolled my eyes at myself. "Sure. Fine. Maybe I felt something like nostalgia. And I couldn't help but notice that he's extremely attractive. Thus, I find him attractive. You've seen his photo online, right? But I don't know him now. How could I have relevant, real feelings for someone I don't know?"

This last rhetorical question seemed to resonate with Kaitlyn because she nodded like my logic passed muster. "That makes sense. Then, proceed. What happened last week?"

"Last week, Andreas showed up at my job, then at my apartment on Friday."

Kaitlyn sat up straighter. "Wait, he's here? In the city? I thought you said he called you."

"No, I said he *contacted* me." I then proceeded to tell her, in the most objective language I could find, about my recent interactions with the Kristiansens and Andreas's offers: the meeting at the café, the sinister visit from Tobias, Andreas's second visit and his last-resort plan to adopt me, complete with all the legal logic and strategic implications.

I watched Kaitlyn's face run the full spectrum of disbelief, delight, then a little concern.

I concluded, "So, basically, if I allow him to adopt me, I will inherit controlling interest in Genetix. Unlike marriage, adoptions are extremely difficult to contest when it comes to inheritance, in part due to intestacy laws."

"Does that count? Isn't Oskar Kristiansen Norwegian?"

"Andreas has dual citizenship, but Oskar renounced his Norwegian citizenship. He's a naturalized US citizen and his personal holdings fall under US law. In the US, adoptions are extremely difficult to reverse, so there would be no going back. And it's not like this is unprecedented. Adult adoption is a common practice used by estate lawyers as a way to circumvent established legacy trusts and limits on inheritance eligibility."

"So, what's the problem?"

"I'm not sure." I rubbed my forehead. "If he adopts me, then—legally—it severs ties with my own biological family, but that doesn't matter. My grandfather and I don't keep in touch and I have no one else left."

She covered my hand with hers and gave it a squeeze. "But, what happens if Andreas adopts you? Is that it? Or does he want anything else? Or is it just, like, he adopts you secretly, you sign the paperwork, you both get on with your lives until Oskar kicks the bucket? And then —BAM! Reveal at the will reading."

"He didn't mention anything about the logistics or additional contact, so I have to assume we sign the paperwork and move on, go back to being strangers." I met her concerned gaze. "Listen, I realize it makes sense. This is my chance. I don't have anything to lose, but it *feels* like I do. It feels like the price is—I don't even know. My dignity? Life as I know it? The space-time continuum?"

Kaitlyn let out a slow whistle, the kind my grandmother would use when she decided to keep her thoughts—but not her judgy whistles—to herself. "This is a lot."

Before either of us could process further, the nursery door creaked, and Martin, six-foot-three former varsity rower, strode into the room. He wore an NYC Club Crew sweatshirt and gym shorts, despite the temperature.

"He's out," he said to his wife, crossing directly to her and bending down to give her a kiss, then staring at her.

After a beat, Kaitlyn frowned at her husband. "Say hi to Sam. Don't be rude."

Martin gave Kaitlyn a small smile, then straightened, his smile disappearing into the ether. "Sam," he said.

"Sandeke," I said with an equivalent amount of warmth.

We weren't frenemies, nor were we friends, nor were we enemies. More like, we tolerated each other's existence for the sake of our mutual adoration for Kaitlyn.

I turned my attention back to Kaitlyn, planning to ask her to help me make a pro / con list, when Martin unexpectedly said, "Andreas's strategy is solid."

I blinked, stunned, and croaked out, "You were listening?"

"Your voice carries. And don't worry. Obviously, I won't tell anyone." He sat down behind Kaitlyn, encouraging her to lean back against him. "You can seal and hide an adoption, but you can't do the same thing with a marriage. Adopting you is a much better strategy than getting married and trying to have a baby. Anything could happen in nine months. Likewise, a sudden marriage between two people who haven't seen each other in years, given your families' history, is suspect. Andreas's brothers would start to dig and discover the addendum to the will, then make their own plans, which would include interfering with yours. I doubt you want your child to be a perpetual target."

"Okay. Noted," I said, reluctantly grateful for his rational assessment of the situation. Martin Sandeke had no skin in the game, he certainly didn't care about me or Andreas. Thus, his impartiality was valuable. Not to mention the man was one of the most inherently shrewd businessmen I'd ever met. "But, to be clear, I have not agreed to be adopted. Yet."

Kaitlyn leaned over and stage-whispered, "But you want to."

I considered this, then hunched forward with the weight of it. "Maybe? I don't know. It would fantastic to screw them over, but also . . . really fucking weird to have Andreas as my adopted *father*." Just thinking about it gave me *Flowers in the Attic* heebie-jeebies, even though I knew it shouldn't. We weren't biologically related, and adult adoption for inheritance purposes wasn't unheard of.

Martin slid his arms around Kaitlyn, drawing her further back. "Let me ask you something, Sam. Do you trust Andreas?"

I didn't even have to think. "Yes."

Martin inspected me for a moment. "You don't trust many people. Why him?"

I picked up my tea. "When we were kids, he always kept my secrets, and I'm the holder of his. Even when it cost him. Even after my dad died, even after the two families went thermonuclear."

Kaitlyn snuggled back against her husband. "You know, Martin and you have that in common. He doesn't trust people, either."

I twisted my lips to the side. "Well, the trust is moot unless I can survive the psychological fallout of being the adopted daughter of my childhood . . ." I struggled for a moment on how to best describe Andreas, finally settling on, "My childhood best friend."

Martin lifted an eyebrow. "You went to law school, you know that's not how the law sees it. There was that famous case a few years ago about that man who adopted his girlfriend to avoid paying out in a civil suit. The primary use of adult adoption is inheritance. Many people adopt their significant other to get around legacy trust inheritance limitations or civil court rulings."

I lifted an eyebrow. "'Many people'?"

"Fine. Many rich people with sizable trust funds. Happy?"

I nodded. "Proceed."

"I'm just saying, an adult adoptee is not in the same category as a child adoptee. It's basically paperwork. Don't let the label psyche you out or keep you from taking what you want. Or, more accurately, taking what it sounds like you deserve."

I already knew and logically understood the difference between adult and childhood adoption. Logic wasn't the problem. *Feelings* were the problem.

Kaitlyn leaned back, her head on Martin's shoulder, and looked at him. "You think Sam deserves Genetix?"

He nodded. "I mean, yeah. After what they did to your family? Why are you hesitating? Just do it. If it were me, I'd jump at the chance to take Genetix from the Kristiansens."

Kaitlyn patted his hand. "I know you would, honey." Then to me she whispered, "He just wishes he had more targets for his revenge plots."

He glowered at his wife from behind her back while I fought a laugh.

"Anyway." Martin gave his attention back to me. "If you do go through with it, you'll need a cover story. Something to distract the rest of the Kristiansens from what's really happening. Your friend, Andreas, he needs to make it look like he's taking some sort of action on the will addendum. Otherwise, the brothers will sniff out the adoption eventually, even if the record is sealed."

I leaned forward, wondering if I should be taking notes. "Like what, exactly?"

Martin's eyes lifted up and to the left. "Like . . . once they discover the addendum to the will, Andreas should pretend to be trying to have a baby with someone. It doesn't have to be you, just someone believable. Or, at the very least, get engaged. That'll keep them distracted."

I blinked. "That's ridiculous. Didn't you just say getting married and having a baby is the weaker strategy? And who would sign up to pretend to be Andreas's fake—" I stopped myself before completing that sentence, because *plenty* of people would line up to be Andreas Kristiansen's fake fiancée.

Just the thought made my stomach sour.

Luckily, Kaitlyn chimed in, "No, actually, that's smart. It *is* the wrong strategy, but that doesn't mean they'll question it. If he makes it look like he's getting together with someone just to have a baby, just to meet the requirements of the will, nobody will suspect that you're already the first grandchild by adoption."

Martin nodded. "Exactly. Give the brothers a plausible red herring."

I squinted at them both. "Is this a normal thing? Am I the only one who thinks this is bonkers?"

Kaitlyn smiled. "Sam, you called me yesterday to say you needed to talk. I assumed it was because you'd finally set the lab on fire. But instead, you're about to execute a legendary revenge plot against the men who ruined your family and become the heiress of a multinational corporation. What is the actual downside? How could I not support this?"

My chest felt weirdly tight, like my heart was expanding but also getting ready to collapse under its own weight. "I haven't agreed to anything yet. I said I needed time to think."

Martin shook his head. "No. You've already made your decision, Sam. You just need to convince yourself you're okay with it."

I thought about that. About the way I kept recalling the words of the will addendum like a prayer; the way I'd memorized the addendum after only reading it twice, every legalese loophole; how I'd researched sealed adoptions using a public library computer browser yesterday morning. I thought about the way I'd spent my entire life pretending I didn't care about what the Kristiansens did, when in fact I'd been quietly dreaming of this exact moment for fifteen years.

"Yeah," I admitted, voice soft. "I want it. I want to make them suffer and lose everything, I want to take back my father's company. I think I'd do almost anything. Even this."

Martin nodded, the movement slow and deliberate. "From my own personal experience, here's what I can tell you. It'll be worth it, so long as you don't lose something—or someone—more important to you in the process."

I looked from him to Kaitlyn, then back at him. "You mean, like how you almost lost Kaitlyn when you went after your own dad?"

He shrugged, like this was old news. "Sometimes you don't know what your priorities are until you're forced to choose."

"And you ultimately chose Kaitlyn over justice," I supplied.

He nodded, looking not at all regretful.

Kaitlyn squeezed his hand. "Let's be honest when among friends. You're both talking about revenge, Sam. Maybe it's also justice, but for you, it's definitely the latter."

"You're right." I shook my head and looked up to the ceiling. "Thank you. For not thinking I'm completely foolish, or irrational."

Martin stretched his legs out on the large leather sofa. "I know you graduated from law school and passed the bar, but if you need a lawyer to draw up an adoption contract with Andreas, let me know. You can use someone from our legal department."

My eyes widened with surprise at his offer. He was correct. I'd graduated from law school and passed the bar, but that was four years ago, a career path abandoned after I realized how much I disliked confrontation and pointless arguments. The only thing I enjoyed about law was the research aspect, and those jobs were being replaced by AI.

"Hey. Thanks, Martin. That's . . . nice of you."

His expression flattened. "You act like I'm never nice to you."

I didn't respond to that, saying instead, "I guess I didn't realize that all it would take for us to truly get along was a little revenge bonding."

He scoffed, but he also sorta smiled.

Kaitlyn, her eyelids drooping tiredly, spoke around a yawn. "I'm not a huge fan of revenge in general, but we're with you, Samwise. Whatever you decide."

The rest of the evening blurred a little. We sat, we drank tea, we talked about everything except the impending plot to upend the Kristiansen hold on Genetix. We ate half a box of lemon cookies and made jokes about how Joey would someday destroy the world by inheriting his father's penchant for revenge and his mother's ridiculous IQ. Eventually, I left, wrapped in a cloud of borrowed warmth and assurance.

On the walk home, I looked up at the dark autumn sky and tried to picture what my life might look like if I went through with it. If I said yes.

I thought about Andreas, about the look on his face when he'd asked me to be his daughter, about the way he'd seemed frustrated about it. Or maybe that was my imagination. Or perhaps I was the one who was frustrated.

Whatever. You've already decided, my brain whispered. *You're just stalling.*

I stopped under a streetlamp, took out my phone, and stared at the new contact labeled simply *Andreas*. My thumb hovered over the call button.

Maybe tomorrow, I told myself, and slipped the phone back into my coat.

The wind was still biting, but I barely noticed.

[9]

INHERITANCE PATTERNS

Samantha

The next morning, I woke up on the blue corduroy sofa in the apartment's family room and I had zero recollection of how I got there.

But I'd had that dream again, the one where Andreas and I were building a banket and pillow fort and we'd turned into adult versions of ourselves. But instead of asking me to marry him, this time Andreas had told me he'd already adopted me. And then right after saying the words, he'd died.

Last thing I remembered before falling asleep last night, I'd been on my bed reading an article about ancient microbiome DNA. I'd been wearing a sleep shirt, undies, and nothing else. Now, I was in jeans and a backward, inside-out T-shirt, sitting on the couch, covered in a chunky fleece blanket that smelled like citrus and old bagels, and someone—probably Diya—had set a glass of water and two ibuprofen on the coffee table in front of me.

I reached for the water, my hand trembling a little, and chugged half the glass before the first wave of disorientation passed. My mouth tasted sour. My arms and legs felt like they'd been disconnected and reattached. I squinted at the clock on the wall: 5:32 AM.

Sleepwalking. Again. I didn't want to think about it, but my brain, like a bad roommate, always ignored closed doors and boundaries.

Instead, it replayed last night's series of decisions, starting with the walk home from Kaitlyn's, followed by the usual ritual of brushing my teeth, setting my alarm, etc. This time, there'd been an addition to the ritual. Sitting on the edge of my bed for a solid forty minutes, staring at my phone and hovering over Andreas's number, willing myself to call and agree to his scheme.

I never did call him. I fell asleep on my bed and now I was here.

Standing, and ignoring the twin protests from my spine and my sense of mental stability, I shuffled to the kitchen for more water. I heard the hiss of the shower from the hall bath and figured Nakita was gearing up for an early shift. I didn't know where Kendra or Diya were, however.

My backpack was on the floor by the front door, right where I'd left it last night. I shouldered it, poured another glass of water, and—after a moment's debate—went to my room and grabbed the towel and shower caddy from my closet, placing them in a duffel bag. I had a huge task list today and I couldn't afford to allow myself to freak out about the troubling reemergence of my sleepwalking.

I simply need—

I needed to start taking better care of myself and avoiding anything in my life that caused stress. And maybe . . . maybe my subconscious knew the right answer before the rest of me did.

* * *

Mostly jogging to work, I made a beeline for the women's locker room. Once there, I showered, scrubbing my skin with more aggression than usual. I tried to lather off all the weirdness and disruption of the last few weeks, tried to wash away the greasy film of sleep deprivation and bad memories.

For once, I used the fancy pomegranate shampoo Diya had given me for my birthday. I shaved my legs, even though it was November and nobody would be seeing them, not even me. I also exfoliated, which I hadn't done since law school.

After drying off, I spent a long moment in front of the mirror, examining my reflection the way a pathologist might examine a suspicious cell line. The usual pale skin, brown hair pulled into a wet bun, blue-gray eyes underscored by dark circles.

I put on the clean underwear set I kept in my locker for emergencies, then my scrubs and lab coat. I even dabbed on a little concealer and mascara since I wouldn't be running any samples in the secure lab today. The makeup made my eyes pop but also hid the dark circles. For the first time in months, I felt a flicker of actual, non-caffeine alertness.

The cotton pants were too short at the ankles, and the shirt was a touch too baggy, but at least I looked and smelled like a functioning human.

I walked the length of the building's main corridor, my sneakers squeaking on the linoleum. My plan was to call Andreas before I got sucked into spreadsheets. I'd decided this in the shower, the same way I sometimes convinced myself to go to spin class. I always seemed to make my most responsible choices while taking a shower, as though good-decision inertia buoyed my motivation and self-control, especially when it came to doing something difficult.

The plan was to call, say, "Thanks, but no thanks," and then block Andreas's number and hope we never ran into each other ever again.

Or at the very least, tell Andreas that, after careful consideration, I'd decided to let the past stay in the past and focus on my future. And then block his number and hope we never ran into each other ever again.

No matter how airtight the legal strategy, no matter how delicious the revenge, no matter how badly I wanted my father's company, I'd spent the last ten years, since I'd turned eighteen, trying to put my past behind me. Turning down the adoption meant I would truly and finally let it all go. If I didn't let it go now, once and for all, then I feared I'd continue to sleepwalk; I'd continue simmering in hurt, disappointment, and anger; I'd allow an obsession in the past to ruin my present and future.

Plus, to a much lesser extent, I couldn't come to terms with the visceral wrongness of Andreas adopting me and me being tied to him forever. There was no denying my attraction to him in the present. And, I finally admitted, there was no denying that a younger version of me had deeply loved and cared for a younger version of him.

That was enough reason to put an end to this. I didn't want to be tied to anyone. Ever.

Silly? Maybe. But also facts. Moreover, my sleepwalking agreed with me. My subconscious thought it was a bad idea and there was no arguing with one's subconscious.

I turned into the hallway that led to my cubicle, intending to find a quiet corner to make the call. Instead, my phone buzzed with a new text. Not from Andreas.

It was from Dr. Hauser, my PI. I stopped in my tracks, thumb hovering over the screen. The message was terse, even for her.

Dr. Hauser: Please see me in my office when you arrive.

My first thought, she wanted to discuss my latest sequencing run. Maybe there was a problem with the dataset?

I squared my shoulders, made a U-turn, and walked to her office. The door was half open, as usual. Inside, Dr. Hauser sat at her desk, typing on her laptop. She wore her hair in a tight French braid and her glasses on a chain around her neck. She looked up as I entered.

"Sam," she said, and gestured to the chair opposite her.

I sat.

She closed her laptop, folded her hands, and looked at me with the steady, intelligent gaze that made her both a brilliant scientist and an intimidating mentor. I'd known her for almost four years now, and in that time I'd never seen her hesitate to do the right thing or take responsibility for a mistake. She was the only person in the department I respected without reservation.

"Is everything okay?" I asked, hoping to get the bad news out of the way first.

She nodded, but her lips pressed into a line. "Sam, I want you to know that I fought for you. I did everything I could."

My heart, already unsettled, performed a backflip. "Fought for me?"

Dr. Hauser sighed. "I'm so sorry to tell you this, but I was informed yesterday afternoon that all my funding, including the Teaching Assistantships, has been suspended, effective immediately."

For a moment, her words didn't parse. They hit my brain like a virus, searching for a receptor dock.

When they finally connected, I said, "But—but—why? What happened?"

She leaned back, glasses dangling from the chain, her fingers steepled. "I have no idea. The dean called and said it was temporary, just for the next six months to a year, but he couldn't give me any other information. The foundation account for my lab is under review."

"That makes no sense," I sputtered. "You're the top grant recipient in the department. You bring in more money than the next three PIs combined."

She shrugged, a sharp, angry motion. "Apparently not for the next six months to a year." She paused, then added, "I'm not the only one. It's department-wide, but for some reason, they targeted my lab and two others first. The other two professors have tenure. I do not."

I stared at her. "So . . . I'm out? I don't understand. I thought the university covered Teaching Assistantship positions once I've been accepted into the program. Isn't that standard?"

"Yes, it should be. I have asked this question and was told that your Teaching Assistantship—specifically—has been placed on hold."

"I've been removed from the program?" My voice pitched high.

"No. That's what doesn't make sense. I don't understand this either and I'll push for more answers. In the meantime"—she picked up a folder from the edge of her desk and slid it toward me—"don't worry. I've spoken with James, and he's agreed to take you on. You might be aware, but his postdoc just left. This won't be a postdoc position, obviously. But he was happy to step in and help."

I picked up the folder, but my fingers barely worked. "James Nieminen?"

"Yes. He's the only one with private funding who can take you on without a gap until we can get answers regarding your Teaching Assistantship and continuation in the program. He'll get you the hours you need, and he's agreed to let you continue your research as a side project, provided you help with his upcoming publication deadlines."

My jaw clenched. I wanted to scream. *Of course.*

Instead, I said, "Will I continue to report to you?"

"Unfortunately, no. Dr. Nieminen will be your PI for the time being. He'll need to have you do some work on his projects to justify the funding through his grants, and—as I said—it won't be a Teaching Assistantship until we can get some answers." She gave her head a quick, frustrated shake. "I apologize. This is a mess. I wish I could give you more information, but I don't understand what's happening either. You might need to get another part-time job elsewhere, and this will likely delay your dissertation."

"Why do you think this happened?"

"I have no idea. Maybe a major donor or alumni called and requested an internal review, or something like that. Honestly, I'm at a loss. I've only seen this happen once before, when a professor angered an important lobbyist and that lobbyist pulled strings in Washington. It's incredibly unusual, but these are unprecedented times."

"I understand," I croaked, confusion giving way to cold certainty, because I did understand. I understood perfectly.

Tobias Kristiansen.

He was responsible.

Hadn't he threatened to do this very thing?

Dr. Hauser watched me for another long moment, then softened, her voice dropping a notch. "Sam, I know this is a setback. But it's not permanent. As soon as everything is sorted, you'll be back working with me, no question."

I nodded. "Thank you."

She smiled, the first time in this meeting. "You're a good scientist. Don't let this stop you."

I stood, folder in hand. "I won't."

Outside her office, I walked the corridor in a straight line, barely seeing the world around me. All I could think was, *This is Tobias. This is Tobias, and this is how he plays dirty. If you won't take the carrot, he'll take the stick to everyone you care about.*

The more I thought about it, the more it made sense. Tobias's threat had been surgical, precise. He didn't even have to pull Kristiansen funding from the department, that would reveal him as the puppet master behind the scenes. He only needed to request a review of funding, not just from my position, but from anyone who he thought might help me. He'd cut off my way forward, and now, if I wanted to finish my PhD within the next decade, he thought I'd have to play by his rules.

The rage was slow and cold, like dry ice. It spread from the base of my skull to the tips of my fingers. I could feel my pulse in my teeth.

If this is how Tobias wants to do things, then I will teach him the definition of playing dirty.

Not only would I allow Andreas to adopt me, and thereby I would inherit the controlling shares in Genetix, I would uncover Tobias's role in framing my father fifteen years ago. I would dig up every single piece of dirt on that asshole and ensure he rotted in prison for the rest of his life.

High on rage, I took out my phone and found Andreas's number.

Samantha: I agree. Let's meet ASAP.

Andreas's response was almost instantaneous.

Andreas: Name the place.

I stared at the screen, my anger settling into a sickly sort of vindication. I would gladly sleepwalk for the rest of my life if it meant exacting revenge on Tobias, Henrik, and Oskar and their accomplices. My subconscious could go take a flying leap.

Tobias didn't want me around Andreas? Fine. Not only would I destroy Tobias, I would strut around with Andreas like a friggin' male peacock, shoving our renewed relationship in that mayonnaise-colored dipshit's face.

Samantha: Text me your address. I'll come over tonight.

A moment later, Andreas's address came through.

I put my phone away and walked to the women's bathroom, locked myself in a stall, and sat on the closed lid. I didn't cry, because I'd stopped crying years ago. Instead, I replayed my conversation with Tobias last week over and over, studying all his threats, analyzing each statement for a potential weakness. When I finished with him, he'd wish he'd never been born.

This was it. This was the moment.

I flushed the empty toilet, left the stall, washed my hands, and went to work.

* * *

If you ever want to know what it feels like to operate your own body on autopilot while your brain runs a continuous background loop of wrath, try waking up to the knowledge that your entire life has been puppeted by two generations of sociopaths, and that your only way out involves being adopted by your former childhood best friend.

I got through the rest of that day like a woman possessed.

Task list: pulverized.

Experimental run: so flawless, I double-checked the calibration because I suspected a supernatural intervention. I'd removed my makeup so I could enter the lab because I had a feeling today was the day those little bastards bent to my will.

Nieminen's hand on my thigh during our "transition review" meeting: ignored. (I set a personal record for not cringing. If this had been the Olympics, I would've gold medaled in Disassociation in a Professional Setting.)

I even survived Dmitry's worried hovering at lunch, where he watched me eat a granola bar in clinical silence and finally asked, "Are you okay?"

"Yes," I said. "Never been better."

He frowned, then returned to his quinoa salad, occasionally shooting me glances as though he expected me to mutate at any moment.

I should've won a fucking Oscar for my portrayal of World's Most Unbothered Grad Student Whose Funding Has Abruptly Ended and Who Has Been Forced to Work for a Sleezy Professor Who Won't Stop Touching Her.

By 5:01 PM, I'd finished my work, closed out my samples, and actually left the building at closing time, a feat unheard of in my department. As I walked down the steps into the blue evening chill, my phone vibrated with an automated reminder that my monthly health insurance payment was due. I ignored it and focused on the plan.

Step one: cash withdrawal.

I hit the ATM, yanking three crisp hundreds from my grandmother's account. I tried not to think about the promise I'd made her ("Don't use this money for anything stupid or self-destructive, like revenge") as I pocketed the bills. Given the events of this morning and the level of Tobias's evilness, I would gladly break this promise. And part of me hoped Grandma would understand. Even if she didn't, nothing would stop me now.

Step two: outfit.

I walked thirty blocks east to a store whose name I will not mention, because it was a discount luxury boutique that only locals know about. The store catered to online influencers and women who had never paid full price for anything, ever. I fit right in, in my faded black jeans and a hoodie that said "I HAVE BACTERIA ON MY MIND." Nobody looked at me twice.

There, I bought a little black dress so tight it looked vacuum sealed, a set of thigh-high stockings in a shade called raven, and a jewelry set composed of black glass drops and gold. The saleswoman said, "Excellent choices," in the dry tone of a former Soviet judge, but she gift wrapped the lot and even threw in a lipstick sample.

Step three: transformation.

Back at my apartment, I locked myself in the bathroom and stared in the mirror for a long time, memorizing my own face. I'd lost weight this semester, and with the way my cheekbones now jutted, I looked faintly starved. *I need to eat more nutritious foods.*

I wiped the remains of the day off my skin, then spent the next forty-five minutes blow-drying my hair, taming it into a glossy, brown-goldish sweep. I applied two layers of makeup. One to erase, and one to repaint. When I zipped myself into the dress, I felt like a different person.

I dug through my closet for my favorite stilettos, the pair I'd bought for a law firm interview and never worn. They were black leather, with a single, elegant ankle strap. I put them on, wobbled once, and then remembered how to walk in three-inch heels.

I added the new jewelry, the shiny drops cold against my collarbone. For the finishing touch, I draped my long, black wool overcoat across my shoulders—open at the front, I didn't want the dress to go unnoticed—and wrapped my grandmother's red-and-pink silk scarf from Paris around my neck for courage.

Staring at myself in the full-length mirror by the door, I didn't recognize the woman who stared back. It was a former version of me, one I thought I'd—sadly—left behind in undergrad. I loved her then, I loved her now, but I'd thought I didn't have much time for her these days.

That changed now.

I wished I could claim that I did this all for myself. I wished this was—at least in part—a way to pamper and take loving care of Samantha Sylvia Jarlston. But this was not the case. I knew I was being watched, and *that* was both the point and the reason for this costume change.

It was all for Tobias Kristiansen. For Henrik. For Oskar, even if the old man was probably hooked up to life support. I wanted them to see me—the version who would walk into their world and burn it down with her bare hands, or at least in heels—and continue to underestimate me.

With one last look in the mirror, I grabbed my clutch (which I'd emptied of everything but an ID, keys, some cash, and a lipstick), and walked out the door.

It was only a fifteen-minute walk to the address Andreas had texted, but the heels made every step feel like a conscious act of defiance. The city was dark now, the wind biting, but I didn't feel cold. In my mind, I pictured the way Tobias would react when he got the report that I'd arrived at Andreas's apartment at this hour despite him cutting my funding.

That thought kept me warm all the way to Andreas's building.

The doorman was a thin man with perfect posture, and when I approached he looked me over once, then gave a tiny, involuntary-looking bow.

"Good evening, miss. May I help you?"

I set my jaw and said, "I'm here to see Andreas Kristiansen."

The man's eyes flickered—maybe at the fact that I didn't introduce myself—but he didn't lose his composure.

He held the door for me. I entered. Once inside, he picked up a corded phone, dialed an extension, then spoke in a low, respectful voice. "I believe the guest you've been expecting, Ms. Jarlston, is here."

The doorman listened, then nodded, then hung up. "He's expecting you. The elevator will take you to the top floor. Straight ahead, then right."

I thanked him, giving the lobby a cursory, but shallow, inspection. The marble glowed gold, and the crystal chandeliers shone in the mirrored paneling like the inside of a jewelry box. The elevator was also mirrored, and as I rode up, I caught myself rehearsing the conversation in my head, rapid-fire, like a verbal chess game.

What was I supposed to say in greeting when I saw Andreas? Maybe, "Hi. Let's destroy your family," or "Welcome to the revenge zone!"

The elevator doors opened into a private vestibule, dimly lit and silent. I took a breath, then walked down the hallway, my heels sharp on the marble.

At the end of the hall, a pair of double doors. I rang the bell.

It took maybe ten seconds for the lock to click and the right door to open. Andreas stood in the entry, backlit by warm light, wearing a light gray dress shirt and a pair of black slacks that probably cost more than my laptop. His hair was damp, as though he'd just showered, and his feet were covered in black socks on the wood floor. The contrast made him look both absurdly formal and completely unguarded.

He looked at me. For a moment, there was nothing else in the world. His eyes—grayish green in the overhead light—swept over me from my hair to my heavy makeup to the open lapels of my coat hinting at the dress beneath to my shoes, then back again.

His lips parted. His eyebrows pulled together. He said nothing, just stared like he'd never seen me before. Or maybe like he was seeing me for the first time.

"May I come in?" I smiled, stepping over the threshold before he could answer. Tugging the scarf from my neck, I rolled it up and stuffed it inside my coat pocket.

"Of course." He closed the door behind me, then stood awkwardly, perhaps unsure what to do next. From what I could see, the apartment was vast, every visible wall covered in paintings and polished wood and midcentury modern—probably Danish—walnut-and-white furniture and antique dark red, hand-knotted rugs. It was exceedingly stylish, and if an apartment could be described as sexy, it was that too. But I fought a smirk because a baby would totally trash this place with their sticky fingers.

Can you imagine? A white couch and a toddler? Yikes.

There were no visible photos, and nothing I recognized that he might've inherited from his family. But there was a chessboard on a big, black, round wooden table. The entire wall of the living room beyond the entry was floor-to-ceiling glass, and the city sprawled outside, an infinite grid of lights.

He offered to take my coat. I shrugged it off, and when he saw the rest of the dress underneath, he made a short sound. When I turned over my shoulder, I caught a glimpse of his wide eyes before he looked away so quickly I almost laughed.

Andreas hung the coat neatly in a closet and returned slowly, standing a polite distance away with his hands shoved in his pockets, his gaze never settling on me for long.

I stared at him, letting him stew in whatever emotion had him looking so entirely disconcerted. He needed to get used to this version of Samantha, because she wasn't going anywhere anytime soon.

His cheeks had turned an adorable shade of pink and his mouth formed a flat, determined line. But then, jaw tight, his eyes finally met and held mine, and only then did I speak.

"Let's get down to business."

ORGANISM REPRODUCTION

Samantha

Andreas's round table in the living room looked like it had been custom-made. It was a dense, glossy black wood, about six feet in diameter, and ringed with matching chairs. At the table's center was a chess set with odd-looking pieces carved out of tan and dark brown wood, arranged in a game that had clearly been abandoned mid-slaughter.

Andreas pulled out a chair for me, pushed it in, then sat opposite. There was a legal-paper-sized envelope on the table with the word "ADOPTION" written neatly across the front. In block letters. Not at all subtle.

I crossed my legs, fighting to keep the hem of my vacuum-sealed dress from inching too high even though the table obscured my lap and legs from view.

"Here it is," he said, placing a pen atop the envelope and nudging both forward with one elegant finger. "Drafted by my attorney. Read it before we proceed."

"When did you have it drafted?" I glanced between Andreas and the folder.

"Before I came to your apartment. I wanted to have it ready as soon as you agreed." He relocated the chessboard to his right, leaving the space between us clear except for the envelope.

"You were so sure I'd agree?" I set the pen to one side and withdrew the document, already skimming the cover letter.

"Not sure. Hopeful."

At his answer, I didn't look up. I settled in to read the adoption packet.

Or rather, I tried to read it. Andreas didn't move, yet the air between us felt dense, charged. I endeavored to ignore it, but the dress I'd worn was having none of my logical resistance. It clung everywhere, making me acutely aware of my body and my pulse. After a full minute, I sensed that while I had my eyes glued to the contract, he had his glued to me.

I looked up.

He didn't avert his gaze.

Instead, he sat there, like a patient wolf in a human suit, eyes unblinking.

Before I could blush or notice how incredibly *fine* Andreas looked tonight, I reminded myself that James Neminem was now my boss because Tobias Kristiansen was a mayonnaise-colored incubus who I'd vowed to destroy until my last dying breath, and noticing Andreas's attractiveness was a pointless distraction and a complication I didn't need or want.

Inhaling a deep breath, I returned my attention to the contract. Sure, it was difficult to focus on the words with him openly staring at me. It had also been difficult to resist the urge to break James Neminem's hand earlier today when he'd set it on my thigh.

Anger helped me concentrate. The legal language was dense, yet even a cursory glance told me it was all very standard and likely taken directly from the forms provided by the State of New York.

The adoption would be sealed and private, and the paperwork contained all the typical template sections I would expect from an adult adoption legal document: *The parties agree to assume toward each other the legal relation of parent and child. Adopting Parent will henceforth treat adoptee as if she were the natural child of adopting parent. Adoptee will henceforth* . . . and so forth about treating each other as natural relatives, plus the stark warning that all ties with my previous parents and biological family would cease to exist once the adoption was approved. Since both of my parents were now dead, this part seemed superfluous.

An addendum contract spelled out that I would not be entitled to any other Kristiansen property, nor would I be financially responsible for Andreas or any of his blood relatives, current or future. Though it would be difficult to enforce, it was, in short, the kind of agreement that attempted to protect both parties and leave no wiggle room for the sort of fuckery that had defined our families' interactions fifteen years ago. But, again, difficult to enforce due to intestacy laws.

Technically, as his adopted child, his family automatically became my family.

Fighting a shiver of revulsion at the thought, I skimmed page after page, noted all the sections I needed to complete, then, as I flipped to the last piece of paper, I glanced up and caught Andreas still watching me with an intensity that made my skin prickle against my will.

There was nothing cold about him now. His gaze lingered on my clavicles, dropped lower, then cut back to my face. When our eyes met, something flickered behind his. This wasn't analytical intensity. This was something sharper and more personal, a sort of slow, simmering heat.

I guessed I wasn't the only one wrestling with an inconvenient attraction.

"Do you want to take a picture?" I asked, not hiding my impatience and needing to break the tension.

"Sure," he ground out.

I snorted a laugh and shook my head at his immediate, but aggressive-sounding, response. "Are you okay?"

His left eyebrow twitched. "Why wouldn't I be?"

"You seem . . ." I searched for the word. "Distracted."

He studied me. "Do you have dinner plans after this?" The question almost sounded like an accusation.

I blinked. "After what?"

He lifted his chin, gesturing at me, at my dress. "You are dressed for dinner, or perhaps an event. Or perhaps you have another engagement after our meeting?"

I looked down at myself. The black dress was sculpted, cut to show my collarbones and cleavage, definitely more than I'd shown in the last four years.

I let a smile show. "If you want to take me out to dinner, just ask."

For the first time since we sat, his expression shifted to something other than smoldering displeasure. "Would you accept?"

"Sure. Why not?" I leaned in. "But for the record, this dress is not for you."

Something sharp and quick flashed in his eyes. "Then who is it for?"

"Your brother." I didn't say which one, because it should be obvious. "He cut off my PI's funding today and for the next six months. I figured, if he wants me to stay away from you, then I'll do the opposite. And I'll make a big show about it."

At my response, his posture seemed to relax and he leaned back in his chair. "This is defiance against Tobias and his threats? To show you will not be bullied." Andreas no longer sounded irritated or aggressive.

"That's right." I collected all the pages of the adoption packet, tapping them upright against the table to tidy the stack. "Do you mind if I have my lawyer look at this?" I asked, keeping my tone light.

"You have a lawyer?"

I shrugged. "I do. Is that a problem?"

He shook his head. "No, not at all. That is . . . good. You should have someone to look out for your interests. Just tell me where to send your copy."

"I'll hand carry it in." I scanned the cover letter again, then looked up at him. "There is one other thing I'd like to discuss, and it's related to the adoption."

His intense but bored mask—the one he'd worn when we first met and also in my apartment—slammed into place. "Proceed."

I found myself smiling at his formality. "Even if we do this adoption thing in total secrecy, it still looks suspicious that you and I are suddenly in each other's lives after a fifteen-year hiatus. Tobias, at least, is already watching me."

He tilted his head the barest degree, eyes lighting with something I could only describe as admiration. "You want to create a diversion."

Martin had said it didn't have to be me, and it probably would've been better—safer for my mental health—if it weren't me, but how could I ask some random woman to feign a relationship with Andreas as a red herring just so I could exact revenge?

Also, logistically, the fewer people who knew about our plan and deception, the better.

"Exactly." I leaned forward, letting the pendant on my new necklace catch the light. "We need a smoke screen. Something to explain why you and I have been meeting."

He stared at me, considering. "What do you suggest?"

I drew a deep breath, then said, "We fake an engagement."

His reaction was fascinating. For half a second, his mask slipped and something complicated flickered in his eyes, too quick for me to decipher. Then it was gone, replaced by that patented patient stillness of his that he wore like a favorite sweater.

"You want to use my original proposal as our smoke screen," he said, "while in reality, we pursue the adoption. This would satisfy the addendum to the will and draw their attention away from our real strategy."

"Exactly." I let the silence stretch. "Do you have a problem with that?"

His answer was instantaneous. "No, not at all. It is a good idea. We should."

"Good. Then—"

"But I have some conditions."

I wasn't surprised, I figured he might. In fact, I'd been waiting for him to discuss stipulations and conditions relating to the adoption contract as well. Andreas was famous in the chess world, and—to an extent—in the non-chess world as well. His fame had a global reach. A sealed adoption coming to light after his father died wouldn't bring him good press, nor would the eventual reveal of a fake engagement.

"Fine." I folded my hands. "Let's hear them."

"If we are to pretend to be engaged, you will need to move in here."

I almost burst out laughing, but he looked so serious that I tried to stifle it. "I'm sorry, what?"

"If we are engaged, logic dictates that we should live together." He made the statement sound entirely reasonable. "Otherwise, it would appear suspicious. My brothers will not believe we are together if we are not living together, and I doubt you have time for fake dates, to make more shows"—he gestured to my dress again—"for their benefit. Living together will save us both time. Otherwise, without evidence of our engagement, they will question it."

I considered this. He had a point, even if it was delivered with all the warmth of a robot reading a weather report. His tone didn't matter, but the pragmatic evaluation and solution to a potential problem did.

Not to mention the possible value of this opportunity for me—and my inconvenient attraction problem—personally. Hadn't I always said, attraction fades fastest with either no exposure or too much exposure? Moving in here, seeing Andreas daily and witnessing all his gross habits, because everyone had gross habits, would certainly cure my attraction to him.

Yes, moving in together was a good idea for many reasons.

"Where would we live? Here?" I glanced around, spotting a hallway behind me, then looked back at him just in time to catch his eyes widen slightly.

"You . . . agree?" He sounded surprised.

"Sure. Your reasoning makes sense. How many bedrooms do you have here?"

"I have three bedrooms. You may take whichever you want."

I squinted at him. "Even the main bedroom?"

He arched an eyebrow, the first real sign of amusement I'd seen since I'd arrived. "If you wish."

Leaning back in my seat, I studied him and his request. Certainly, exposure to Andreas never putting the toilet seat down or cleaning up after himself would solve my attraction problem quite nicely. Or, conversely, maybe he was an anal-retentive control freak and couldn't handle a pair of socks on the ground for five minutes. Either would suit me just fine. Then my brain and my body could friend-zone him with no issue.

Logistically, however, moving in here would be complicated. What about my roommates? I couldn't simply leave without finding my replacement. And would I still pay rent in the meantime? What happened when people discovered he'd adopted me? This felt messy.

I must've taken too long to reply because Andreas leaned forward and placed his elbows on the table, asking, "What worries you?"

"I think it would be wise for us to define our concerns and conditions now. In fact, what if we both made a list, about the adoption and the fake-fiancé arrangement?"

"That is agreeable, as long as we set a goal to have everything finalized within three days."

"Why three days?"

He tapped his fingers on the table, a movement that looked absent-minded. "I have been alerted my father's will might be shared with my brothers next week."

"Might be?"

Andreas dipped his chin. "My contact did not provide any other details. Only that we need to move quickly, if we are going to do this."

"Okay, then. No time like the present." Flipping over the cover letter, I picked up the pen and began writing. "I'll jot down my immediate concerns and conditions now. You should get a piece of paper and do the same."

He made a small sound that could've been a laugh or a sigh, but then stood and left the table, only to return a moment later with his own pen and paper.

My list was already quite long:

1) Giving my roommates notice before breaking my rental agreement with them (I still have 8 months).

2) I have to find my own replacement for Diya/don't want to leave her hanging.

3) How much is rent on this place?? Can't afford rent on two apartments. Need breakdown of rent, utilities, etc. for this apartment.

4) How public to go with fake-fiancé agreement? Public PDA as evidence of smoke screen? How much? Rules around PDA seem like a good idea. Related, see number 5.

5) Won't it be weird for you when people find out you've adopted me but we've been acting like we're dating? How's that going to work for your image? Hire a PR firm?

6) Your brother threatening me: If I eventually lose my funding, I might not be able to pay rent here. Need plan for this.

7) Rules for the apartment? Bringing people over? Cleaning duties? Can I have shelves in the fridge and pantry? What rooms can I use?

8) What are you like to live with? Do I need to be quiet during certain hours? What do I need to know about being your roommate?

Reading back over the list, I frowned, because a very obvious thing was missing. Deciding that we were both adults and it would be better to spell things out and be honest than hope everything just magically worked out, I added:

9) No physical contact unless it's in public and only for the purposes of reinforcing the claim that we're engaged. No avoidable contact in the apartment at all and—

"That many?"

Andreas's question pulled my attention away from the list and I glanced at his paper, which—from where I sat—only appeared to have three items.

Setting my pen down, I slid my paper toward him. "This is as many as I can think of right now. I like to have everything clearly spelled out before making a decision. Setting realistic expectations from the beginning will save frustration and disappointment later."

"Are you expecting me to disappoint you, Samantha?" His eyebrow raised slightly. He also slid his paper toward me while accepting my list.

I picked up his paper, not caring how my cleavage pressed against the neckline of my dress—or how his eyes darted to my chest then quickly away—as I reached forward with my fingertips.

He needed to get used to me being in his space in various states of clothed. Roommates had to deal with that kind of stuff.

"I am not expecting you to disappointment me, Andreas. Not if we set realistic expectations."

His eyes narrowed marginally, then shifted to my list.

I glanced at his. He hadn't numbered it.

Samantha moves in with Andreas.

Samantha will have one or more bodyguards.

Samantha will not speak to the press about Andreas; Andreas will not speak to the press about Samantha.

My mouth dropped open at the second item. "Excuse me? A bodyguard?"

Andreas lifted just his eyes and stared at me with a bleak sort of intensity. "You underestimate my brothers. Tobias is ruthless, but he prefers psychological warfare. Henrik is unpredictable and often resorts to physical violence. If we are to publicly pretend that we are a couple, you will become a target. I do not want your safety to be jeopardized."

I inspected him, endeavoring to parse whether he believed a guard was truly necessary.

Before I could push the issue, he shook his head. "This is nonnegotiable."

Letting his succinct list fall to the table, I sat back and crossed my arms. "Then I have a counteroffer."

He watched me, waiting.

"The guard can follow me home from work, or be nearby if I'm out at night, but they can't come into my office, my lab, or anywhere else on campus. For one thing, it would be incredibly awkward, and for another, they don't have the necessary clearance or training to enter the lab."

He considered, then nodded. "Acceptable."

Frowning, I gave him a single nod. "Fine. Bodyguard is approved.

But then"—I reached forward, my palm up—"I need to add more to my list."

He gave me one slow blink. "Just tell me. I will write it for you."

"Who will pay for the bodyguard?"

Andreas seemed to contemplate me for a long moment before setting down my paper. "I propose, for all the expense-related items, we split the cost of everything—lawyers' fees, living expenses, bodyguard, and so forth—fifty-fifty, after you inherit Genetix. For now, I will shoulder all financial burdens."

I turned my head slightly to the side and examined him. "What if our plan fails and I don't inherit?"

"Then I will accept the financial fallout and cover the cost of everything."

"Why would you?" As I asked the question, I wondered again how this arrangement benefited Andreas. Why approach me at all? Was this actually about correcting an injustice? If so, then wouldn't it make more sense for me to cover all the expenses should we succeed rather than split everything fifty-fifty?

"This is my idea, all of it. And I approached you. Of course I should be the one to take the financial responsibility." He said this like it was the most obvious thing in the world.

Still, it didn't sit right.

"Tell me something, Andreas."

A pause while he stared at me in solemn silence, then, "Anything." He sounded entirely sincere, his tender tone completely at odds with the mask of boredom donning his features.

"Why? Why are you doing this? What are you getting out of it? You say you're going to take financial responsibility, but why? As I've spelled out on my list of concerns, won't this whole thing make bad press for you when it comes to light? The woman you've been pretending to date is actually your adopted daughter? That sounds like a scandal."

As I spoke, his gaze grew more distant, reserved. But when I said the word *daughter* he made a face of distaste. "You will not be my 'daughter.'"

"In the eyes of the law, I will be. It says you and I will treat each other like natural—"

"In the eyes of the law, you will be my direct inheritor and the first grandchild of Oskar Kristiansen." He spoke over me.

"Okay, fine. Semantics. But you still haven't answered my question." I pressed my index finger against the first page of the adoption packet. "Why bother doing this at all? Why reach out to me after fifteen years? Why not ask a woman you fancy to make a baby with you, then let your real child inherit?"

"Did I not—" he began, but then clamped his mouth shut and exhaled through his nose, his stare mutating into a glare. After a few more rises and falls of his chest, he spoke. "It should go without saying, what my family did to you and your parents was reprehensible. My father literally stole everything from your family. Genetix should be yours. How could I live with myself if I let this opportunity pass by? Isn't that reason enough?"

Biting the inside of my lower lip, I scrutinized the remoteness of his expression and the coolness of his words, which all seemed to support my previous hypothesis: Andreas was doing this because he cared about justice, and approaching me was merely about righting a past wrong. Granted, it was a big fucking past wrong.

"Huh," I said, feeling oddly disappointed by his answer. But at least I knew for certain the source of his motivations. "Well then, how about this: If we fail, you cover all the expenses. But if we succeed, I cover all the expenses."

"Why not split—"

"That's my final offer." I sat back in my chair again. "I'll move in here and you'll foot the bill for the apartment and living expenses, you pay for the bodyguard, and so forth, because we both know I can't. That answers a lot of my questions and concerns about the logistics. But if we succeed, I pay you back for everything. Take it or leave it."

The calculating quality had reentered Andreas's gaze. "This offer sounds unnecessarily transactional. As though you are paying me for services rendered."

I shook my head. "No, I am *reimbursing* you for services rendered. There's a difference."

As if at all possible, his features grew colder, and I was reminded of that infamous meme of Andreas, staring at an opponent over a chessboard, with the words: "My mouth may not say it, but my face definitely will."

Yeesh. If I didn't have memories of him bawling over the cadaver of a baby bird, he might've been sort of scary right now.

Finally, after a prolonged period of frosty contemplation, he said, "Then I have more conditions."

I picked up my pen, poised to add another item to his list. "What's that? I'll add it for you."

Folding the piece of paper with my list on it in half, he gave his head a slight shake and stood. "No. We will discuss over dinner tomorrow. In the interim, I will write down my additional conditions along with responses to yours. The summary of 'realistic expectations' will be finalized at that time."

Attempting to stand as gracefully as possible given the tightness of my dress, I shrugged. "Fine. But it'll have to be a late dinner. I have a meeting tomorrow evening with my—uh—work colleague." James Nieminen had requested that we meet tomorrow at 6:00 PM. Who schedules a meeting at 6:00 PM on a Friday night? Such a dick move.

"No problem. What time shall I arrange the car?" His tone was solicitous and soft, once more at odds with the frostbite of his stare.

"You'll meet me at my work?"

"Yes." His gaze moved over me again, his expression still calculating. "I will send over something for you to wear and I will make sure the table is by the window."

"Okay. Then seven thirty should be fine." I slid the adoption packet back in the envelope and picked it up. "And I'll take this to my lawyer."

"Let me know if you require any changes to that as well. My attorney is flexible." Andreas adjusted the chessboard he'd pushed aside earlier back to the center of the table.

I nodded, momentarily mesmerized by his long, elegant fingers resetting the pieces, and said without thinking, "That's a pretty chess set."

He met my gaze briefly. "Would you like to play a game before you leave?"

I eyed the board. "Only if you promise not to go easy on me."

His hand holding the black queen paused for a beat before he placed her on a dark square. Lifting his eyes to mine, a faint smile curved his mouth. "I never go easy on anyone."

"Really?" I tilted my head to the side and set a hand on my hip. "You used to be such a softy."

Andreas shoved his hands in his pockets, his gaze never leaving mine, and said quietly, "Only with you."

I made a face of disbelief, but let his comment go. He used to be a softy with nearly everyone. All the staff in his father's house had babied him because he was so sweet. Maybe he liked to think of himself as tough and intimidating now—and no doubt his cold stares absolutely were—but I'd likely never stop seeing flashes of the sensitive, soft boy he used to be.

The one I loved.

Tensing at the thought, I tore my eyes away from his and gave myself a mental shake. "Right. Well. Let me get out of your hair."

Pointing then walking toward the entrance, I wracked my brain trying to remember where he'd put my coat when I arrived, ignoring the tingling sensation running down my spine at the sound of his steps behind me. Once I reached the entrance, I sorta spun in a circle until I found the closet.

Not looking at him, I pulled my coat from the hanger where he'd left it. "I guess I'll see you tomorr—"

Andreas was suddenly next to me, taking my coat and helping me put it on. Then he reached inside the closet and withdrew another coat, the camel-colored cashmere one from the time he'd cornered me outside of my department building so many days ago.

"What are you doing?" I watched him push his arms through the sleeves.

He glanced at me, then pulled out a pair of slip-on, yet exceedingly fancy-looking, black loafers. "I'm walking you home."

"Why are you—"

Feet now ensconced in shoes, Andreas stepped close, pulled my grandmother's scarf from the pocket where I'd stuffed it earlier, and draped it around my neck. He then turned and grabbed the doorknob. "What kind of fiancé would I be if I allowed my future wife to walk home alone at this hour?"

I stared at him and his aloof expression, contemplating his terse-sounding words while he opened the door.

"You know," I said, "I walk around the city by myself all the time, even late at night."

"And?"

I rocked back on my heels. "So, I know how to keep myself safe. You don't think Henrik is already planning an offensive, do you?"

"No. But this is not just about safety." He gestured for me to go first.

Exiting his apartment, I asked over my shoulder, "Then what's it about?"

He pulled his door closed and it beeped. "Never too early to make our relationship appear real. As your soon-to-be fiancé, I will use this and every opportunity."

Confused, I frowned at his profile, then at his back as he walked around me and pressed the call button for the elevator. "Use for what?"

He glanced at me, a hint of incredulousness pulling his eyebrows together. "Samantha, people who want to marry each other usually also want to spend as much time together as possible."

"*Ohhhh.*" I walked forward slowly to stand next to him. "Yeah, of course. I know that."

He sorta smirked, the incredulousness persisting, and faced the elevator doors.

A sensation of unease prickled down my spine. I'd always ended my situationships if or when the guy started doing these types of things. Calling me or texting me frequently, wanting to hang out every day, telling me about his feelings, hopes, or dreams. No matter how upfront and transparent I'd been about my lack of interest in a committed relationship, this sometimes happened. Not every time, but sometimes.

How funny. Now I'd have to do it with Andreas. And it was all fake.

The elevator dinged, announcing its arrival, and again he gestured for me to go first. I did, and then pressed the lobby button. He stepped in next to me and we stood quietly as the elevator descended, the same thick energy from before in his apartment making the surrounding air feel heavy while I actively avoided the sight of our reflection in the paneled mirror.

At least, it felt heavy to me. It felt like hasty decisions and a precursor to regret. But it also felt like a means to an end and the beginning of my revenge against his family, and that's what I focused on. All of this charged atmosphere and these awkward elevator rides would be worth it, in the end.

As the doors slid open revealing the lobby, I moved to exit. Before I could, Andreas smoothly slid his palm against mine and entangled our fingers, making my heart stutter and my feet stumble at the sudden, electric contact. Just like at the café, a jolt of something warm traveled up my arm at his touch and I struggled against the instinct to prolong the contact. This inability to pull away meant I allowed him to grasp my hand and lead me out of the elevator, the lobby, and the building. The doorman I'd spoken to earlier might've greeted us. But I didn't hear what he said.

I continued being led by Andreas down the sidewalk for two blocks before I finally found my voice and whispered, "Why are—must we hold hands?"

"Do you want the smoke screen to look real?" He spared me a side-eye.

I sighed, resolving to add a new condition to my list when we met tomorrow: *Plot out every incidence of PDA before it occurs in order to mitigate prolonged contact. And absolutely no kissing!*

My stomach twisted at the thought of kissing Andreas. I shivered.

He looked at me. "Cold?"

Obviously, I wouldn't explain. I nodded.

Eyes skating over my upturned face, Andreas lifted my hand in his grip and put both of ours in the pocket of his coat, giving my fingers a squeeze. "Better?"

I caught a whiff of rosemary, which I now assumed must've been his shampoo, and nodded again with a small, tight smile as I thought, *No. Worse. Much, much worse.* The man was painfully handsome, and he smelled so good, and his hand felt so good and strong and warm. And this was torture.

But this torture would be worth it, in the end.

[11]

GENETIC VARIATION

Samantha

The biology building felt extra haunted after dark. Tonight, being the Friday night before Thanksgiving week, it was all but abandoned.

A chemical lemon scent trailed behind the janitorial staff, and the green exit signs burned with a weird radioactive intensity. By the time I packed up my notes and shut down the projector in the conference room, it was 6:55 PM and the only light came from the glass-walled corridor outside. Enough to make the space dim, but not bright.

Dr. Nieminen sat across from me, shoes planted just wider than his knees, pecking something into his laptop with two fingers. I'd expected him to try some uninvited shoulder squeeze, or maybe a breathy "Can I get you a drink, Sam?" as soon as he arrived for our 6:00 PM meeting, but he'd been nothing but professionally friendly all meeting, a pleasant surprise.

The most personal statement Dr. Nieminen made thus far was, "I'm told the venue is cold, so bring a sweater." I even caught myself letting my guard down toward the end of my presentation. My notes from the meeting—mostly reminders to email the poster draft to the co-authors, asking for their citation lists and preferred schedule for presentation times—were scrawled with my normal legible handwriting, not the aggravated micro-script I used when forcing myself to concentrate.

Dr. Nieminen's entire agenda this evening had centered on the conference next month in Boston. So, an actual agenda. And one I was prepared for because I'd drafted a presentation last month just in case Dr. Hauser had wanted me to attend and present.

Presently, eyes still on his laptop, he said, "Your presentation is fine, but I want it in abstract format. For the poster, we'll need to unify our graphics, make sure everyone's using the latest template, fonts, and so forth."

I nodded.

"And I'll rely on you to check everyone's citations, make sure they're not taking any shortcuts. Oh! And Dr. Merkle is extremely anal about kerning, especially for titles and diagrams. Sorry."

"Understood." I scribbled another note, *Check letter spacing.*

"I want to thank you, Sam, for how quickly you've adapted to the change in circumstance." Dr. Nieminen finished whatever he was typing, snapped his laptop closed, and smiled at me, that confident, square-jawed American smile he used in all his lab group photos. "I was worried you'd need more time to adjust, but you're approaching your new duties with such, ah—" He paused, as if consulting an internal thesaurus. "Enthusiasm. It is admirable."

I gave him a tight smile, my stomach tense, not because there was anything wrong with the compliment, but because there was *nothing wrong with the compliment.* I genuinely couldn't process the lack of an ulterior motive.

"Thanks," I managed, twisting my pen between my fingers. "It's all pretty similar to what I was doing for Hauser as her research assistant, just with more, you know, product."

He laughed. "You mean more work."

I offered a slightly wider smile. "But more work means more experience, so I'm not complaining."

Dr. Nieminen stacked his laptop, his notebook, and his phone into a tidy, rectangular pile. He then stood, slinging a backpack over his shoulder. "You say that now, but just wait until you see what international peer review is like. It's nothing but stress and disappointment." His tone was dry, but not unkind. "Anything else before we go?"

"No, I think I have everything for now. I'll let you know if the conference organizers need anything else from our end." I almost added, *Thank you for taking me on, for helping me keep some funding at the university*, but caution won out and I decided against vocalizing any gratitude. I didn't trust that his motives were altruistic yet, despite how straightforward and professional he'd been during this meeting.

"Excellent." Dr. Nieminen picked up his stack of items and gripped them to his chest. "What do you think about making our usual meeting time six on Fridays? It seems like the only time the conference rooms are available. Are you free Friday evenings?"

"Usually, yes. That works for me."

"Great. Then I'll see you later." His grin was pleased. "I won't be here next week, visiting my parents for the holiday. Oh yeah. Happy Thanksgiving by the way."

"Thank you. Happy Thanksgiving."

"Any plans?" His head tilted slightly to one side.

"Nothing major," was all I felt comfortable admitting even though I planned to come in every day and take advantage of the empty lab over the holiday. Dr. Nieminen and I weren't friends. Even if we were, I tended to err on the side of caution when sharing details with anyone other than Kaitlyn.

Yeah, yeah. I know. I have trust issues.

With a quick smile and friendly wave, he left.

Meanwhile, I was left frowning at his departing form, feeling slightly adrift. And muddled. But also relieved he hadn't done or said anything that made me uncomfortable. *Maybe I've been unkind. Maybe he's not . . . so bad.*

Eventually, I turned to gather my things, surprised by the direction of my thoughts. This whole situation with Andreas, his brothers, and the addendum to Oskar Kristiansen's will left me twisted in knots.

Last night, Andreas walked me all the way up to the door of my apartment. I told myself it was for appearances, for the benefit of anyone Tobias had sent to follow or photograph us. However, no one was photographing us inside the stairwell of my apartment building, and yet I'd held his hand the whole time. His fingers were warm, and his palm was large and it fit mine so perfectly that letting go had been quite difficult.

Which was why, when I saw him tonight for our late dinner, I was going to insist on a list of acceptable public displays of affection and have them all written down and signed off on. But not notarized. Notarizing that kind of list would be weird. However, I wasn't about to get blindsided again by random hand holding.

Thus, and in retrospect, perhaps I'd overreacted about or misunderstood Dr. Nieminen's hand on my thigh yesterday. *Maybe he's just a touchy-feely guy . . . ?*

I rolled my eyes at myself. He wasn't just a touchy-feely guy. James Nieminen had been interested in me for a while, that was no secret. But perhaps he'd finally taken the hint and decided to back off now that he was my boss and signed off on my paychecks. It seemed possible I was the problem and saw villains where none existed.

Fine. As long as Dr. Nieminen continued to be professional—like today—I would do my work diligently and we would have no problems. But if he crossed the line again, I'd add his name to my People I'm Going to Ruin list, right below Tobias Kristiansen's.

I'd always considered myself an exceptionally pragmatic person, even when I was a child and the other kids on my block wanted to play "wedding" or "FBI" or whatever. I preferred more constructive games, like researching all the pharmaceuticals in my parents' medicine cabinet, or creating elaborate natural disaster scenarios for my Barbie dolls to understand concepts like lava flow, structural integrity of buildings during earthquakes, or the impact of hurricane-force winds on an elaborate hairstyle. The only time I ever did anything truly irrational was when I let myself believe, for a six-month period in middle school, that if I were simply attractive enough, if I wore cute enough clothes and did my hair and wore makeup, I'd feel happy and all my problems would be solved.

That delusion had returned with a vengeance tonight.

After I quickly showered, I blow-dried my hair upside down to maximize volume, then flat-ironed it in sections so that it fell, glossy and heavy, over my left shoulder. Then I did my makeup—full, maximalist mode, with shimmery eyeshadow and a perfect, lethal cat eye. I even did the thing with the contour and highlighter, which I'd watched an online tutorial for back in undergrad and practiced until I'd perfected it.

The dress itself was a slinky, bloodred silk that looked like it should be on a Bond girl. It had been a gift from Andreas. Well, not really a "gift," but a mission-critical apparatus. It arrived by courier in a box with a typed note that read: *Wear tonight. I will match. —A*

The color, a deep burgundy, made my skin appear even paler than usual. I couldn't decide whether the paleness looked good or bad. Either way, the contrast of colors was definitely dramatic.

The cut of the dress was both elegant and indecent in the way that only ultraexpensive things can be. The hem stopped mid-thigh, the neckline was low but not slutty—sadly—and when I zipped myself in, I could feel the silky fabric hugging the curve of my hips and thighs like a second skin.

I put on the same black stilettos I'd worn last night, mostly because I was broke and couldn't justify new shoes. Underneath, I wore the nicest underwear set I owned, the bra so delicate and lacy that it should've been classified as "wishful thinking" rather than an actual undergarment.

As I got dressed, I thought about the fact that tomorrow I'd wake up and it would all be the same. I'd still be broke, still fighting to keep my place in the program, still obsessing about how to make the Kristiansens suffer. But tonight, with the clock ticking down to the first of potentially many public dinners with Andreas, my lips painted to match the dark red of my dress, I was going to enjoy myself. I deserved a break, a treat (that wasn't ice cream) to celebrate the fact that I'd fully embraced my revenge era.

*Rather, a treat that didn't involve *just* ice cream.*

By the time I finished, I felt good. Energized. *Ready.*

Slipping on my black coat, I grabbed the envelope with the finalized adoption contract. Martin had been kind enough to send his lawyer over for a breakfast meeting with me this morning and we'd completed all the details over coffee at the fake-foliage café across the street. Checking the screen of my phone, I saw it was 7:25 PM. I had enough time to get to the curb and collect my wits before Andreas's car arrived.

The hallways in the biology building were now totally deserted, echoey in the weird way only abandoned academic buildings get. When I stepped out into the street, the air was sharp and so dry it stung my nose. The sky was clear and the streetlamps bled orange halos onto the concrete. At the far curb, a black Mercedes SUV idled, windows tinted to near-opacity. I squinted at it, wondering if this SUV could be Andreas.

Obviously, I wouldn't approach without confirmation. Only dumb Marty Sues and Mary Sues walk toward mysterious idling, black Mercedes SUVs.

Instead, I checked my phone. No new messages. Sliding it back into my clutch, I scanned the sidewalk and decided I would text Andreas after five more minutes. To my right, in the shadows cast by the building's decorative columns, something flickered in the corner of my vision. Movement.

I tensed, scanning the darkness. But then, when I saw nothing, I relaxed. Except, I looked again. And I could've sworn I saw a flash of blue. The same blue as the jacket Dr. Nieminen had worn earlier.

I frowned. Why would Nieminen be here? The man was a machine, but even he didn't keep office hours this late on a Friday, especially not the Friday before Thanksgiving. Maybe he'd forgotten something and had come back to get it? Or maybe—my skin crawled—a completely unrelated creep was lurking outside the biology building.

I debated for a full five seconds whether to call over and say,

"James, if that's you, you're being a weirdo," but I didn't want to risk being wrong if it were a lurking stranger.

Instead, I turned away from the column, preparing to text Andreas that I'd arrived, when I heard my name.

"Samantha."

It was Andreas's voice, unhurried and flat, but pitched lower than usual.

I looked up. He stood at the rear of the Mercedes I'd noticed earlier. Relieved and grateful that he was already here, I walked toward him.

Andreas watched me approach and, as I drew closer, I saw that his black overcoat was open, revealing a suit. I suspected it was the exact color of the dress he'd sent me, a dark burgundy, with a black shirt underneath. Once again, he looked like he'd been peeled off the cover of an Italian fashion magazine. Maybe that was deliberate, but it still made my brain short-circuit for a second.

There was something almost aggressively attractive about how much he didn't smile, or blink, or do anything besides track my every movement with his intelligent eyes.

I stopped just short of him. "Uh, nice suit," I said as neutrally as possible.

His eyes flicked down my body, mostly hidden by my black coat, then back to my face. "Did you get the dress?"

Unbuttoning the front of my jacket, I held open one flap to show him a peek of the sheath dress beneath.

His glanced away, clearing his throat before saying, "A simple yes would have sufficed."

I almost laughed. Not because it was funny, but because his cheeks were now pink and I didn't think it was from the cold.

I think he likes me . . . Hmm.

No. More accurately, *I think he likes the way I look.* No worries. Once we moved in together and he was exposed to all my weird, disgusting habits, I felt certain any and all attraction to me would fade.

Buttoning my coat, I drifted closer. "Are we on time?"

He checked his watch. "We have exactly eighteen minutes. Please."

Andreas motioned toward the car with a little wave of his hand, giving the open back door of the Mercedes a wide birth.

I walked forward and let myself in, scooting all the way over to the seat behind the driver. Inside, it was warm, and the faint smell rosemary tickled my nose—*Andreas's shampoo*—along with expensive cologne.

Shoving away this recognition—that I now knew what Andreas's shampoo smelled like—I glanced up and met a pair of pretty eyes in the rearview mirror. The driver was a woman. I blinked.

She had light brown hair and, from what I could see of it, a pleasant, open face. The woman looked to be around my age, maybe a few years younger.

"Hi," I said, uncertain of the protocol for greeting a driver who wasn't operating a taxi or a ride-share.

She turned over her shoulder and looked back at me, her eyes crinkled with a smile. "You must be Samantha. I'm Tara."

I blinked at her again. She . . . sorta looked like me. Actually, she looked a lot like me.

"Tara will be your driver," Andreas said, sliding in behind the passenger seat and shutting the door. He didn't glance at me as he spoke. "She is also one of your new bodyguards."

"Nice to meet you, Tara." I moved to the edge of the seat and offered my hand for a shake.

She took it. "You too." Tara grinned, then faced forward.

Andreas's finger hovered over a panel set in the door. "To the restaurant, please."

Tara nodded, then pulled away from the curb, merging the car into traffic so smoothly I barely felt the movement.

Andreas pressed a button on the panel and a sheet of privacy glass lifted, separating us from Tara. Once it was in place, silence engulfed us for a minute, which was fine by me. I took the time to fish my contract envelope out of my purse, smoothing my hands over the exterior.

After a few blocks, Andreas glanced over briefly, the lines of his profile perfect enough to be an ancient Roman statue. He reached into his coat and produced a single folded sheet of paper.

"Answers to your conditions." He held it out.

I took it, instantly noting the neat, precise block handwriting. I scanned down the list, seeing my own words summarized, followed by his responses, each numbered and concise.

1) & 2) Giving notice to roommates and finding replacement: Do whatever is necessary. But you need to move into my apartment within the next three days.

3) Rent and expenses: Already resolved. I pay unless you successfully inherit. In which case, you reimburse.

4) PDA rules: To be discussed.

5) Concerns regarding my public persona: Since what we are doing is not illegal, it will not impact my career in any substantive or adverse way.

6) Threats: I will cover any loss of employment or related expenses due to my family's behavior, including previous financial commitments, student loan repayments, etc.

7) Apartment boundaries/ rules: Full use of all shared living spaces. Guest policy will be determined together. Cleaning and chores: Not required. I have a service.

8) Living with me: I don't know. I've never lived with anyone before. Quiet hours to be discussed.

9) No physical contact unless necessary for public display: Acceptable.

Beneath this numbered list of my conditions, Andreas had written his three conditions from last night along with one new one: *Our engagement must be public and take place ASAP.*

I looked at him, holding the paper in both hands. "This all looks more or less fine. We can negotiate the guest policy and quiet hours, I have no problem with that. And I can move into your place within three days, maybe even this weekend. That shouldn't be an issue since Thanksgiving is next week and it's a slow time of year. But while 'no touching when we're alone' is here and you've agreed it's acceptable, you wrote 'to be discussed' next to the public displays of affection stipulation. What—specifically—needs to be discussed?"

He turned toward me fully, the movement casual but focused. "I fully agree with the sentiment, but we need to discuss the details of our public displays of affection."

"What—what does that mean? You agree with the 'sentiment'?"

"I agree, a strategy for public affection, discussed and defined prior to planned public excursions, seems most efficient. In order to avoid" —his eyes flicked over me—"surprises. If you agree, I will run my suggestions by you for this evening before we arrive."

I blinked. "You already have a list of suggestions for tonight?"

One corner of his mouth curved upward. "You underestimate how often people photograph me in public. It would be suspicious if we never touched, but it would also be suspicious if we went overboard. We must strike the correct balance."

I stared at him, impressed and maybe a little annoyed that he'd already thought all of this through.

"Okay." I refolded the paper. "What are your suggestions for tonight?"

"First, in general, for all outings, I suggest frequent hand holding. At any public dinner for example, I may put my hand over yours and vice versa. If we walk in or out of a venue, I will offer my arm or place a hand on your back. That is it."

My eyes widened. "Wait. That's it?" Why was my stomach sinking?

"Yes. I will never initiate any additional public displays of affection without your advance agreement, and I ask the same of you. If you wish to initiate without prior agreement, I give you permission to do so at your discretion, but please give me a signal first so I am prepared."

I stared at him, nonplussed. "You've seriously thought about all this." For some reason, in addition to my sinking stomach, my neck felt hot. Like I was embarrassed. But I wasn't embarrassed. In fact, I didn't know what I was.

"I have," he said evenly. "I do not want either of us to be uncomfortable. If we are not at ease, our act will not be convincing."

There was a pause. The car slowed as Tara navigated a turn, then merged back into traffic.

I needed to say something, so I asked half jokingly, "Are you always this thorough?"

He tilted his head. "Always."

"Mmm. That's, uh, good. That's good to know." I glanced out the window, watching the city lights streak by while I wrestled with a wave of emotion I didn't understand.

Why did I feel like I'd just been rejected? Truly, my brain made no sense. I'd been the one who wanted to define acceptable PDA. I should be relieved.

"Does that sound acceptable?" Andreas asked after a time. "Any concerns?"

I shook my head, glancing at him then back out the window. "Nope. That sounds good. Good talk."

My reflection in the glass looked weirdly alien, the makeup and my earlier confidence all floating above my own skin like an overlay. I wondered if that's how he saw me, too. Something constructed, but also functional. A girl-shaped object. I was tempted to ask him, but the words stuck in my throat.

For a while, neither of us spoke.

Then, out of nowhere, he said, "There is one more thing to discuss."

I turned forward, bracing myself to face him again. "What's that?"

"We should decide on the appropriate PDA for tonight, as it is a special circumstance."

"Is it?" I gathered a deep breath, then met his gorgeous, half-lidded eyes.

"Yes." He nodded once. "I am going to propose to you tonight."

[12]

HUMAN GENETICS

Samantha

I choked, actually choked, on the nothing I was breathing and stared at him with shocked, wide eyes. "I'm sorry, what?"

Andreas simply looked at me, unblinking, totally serious. "We are having dinner at Maison Lavande. It is a favorite spot of my family's, and they will expect something significant to occur."

"But—but why so fast? Couldn't we—"

"My brothers will imminently know about the addendum to my father's will. It is possible they already know. If I wait, it will look suspicious. If we hurry, it will seem real."

"Then can't we just say we're engaged?"

"I added a public engagement to the list as my final condition." He gestured to the folded paper on my lap. "The more public the proposal, the more difficult it will be for anyone to question it later."

My brain fought to find fault in his statements. Unfortunately, all his points were good ones.

But discomfort also meant I felt compelled to tell a joke. "Okay, I agree, but only if there's an obscenely ostentatious ring involved."

"Yes, I have it here"—he patted his side pocket, clearly not comprehending my attempt at humor—"but you do not have to wear it unless you wish to. The size of the spectacle tonight will be in accordance with your comfort level."

I couldn't seem to form words as I watched Andreas reach into his pocket and produce a small, navy blue velvet box. He set it on the seat between us.

I stared at it, then at him, then back at the box. "Uh, well. I guess . . ." I scratched my neck. "I'm sorry, could you repeat the question?"

His eyes narrowed, but he sounded infinitely patient as he spoke. "What level of PDA, and spectacle, are you comfortable with tonight? I have reserved the entire restaurant. Flowers, a cake, champagne, candles, rose petals, and musicians are planned. The waitstaff will be our witnesses and our table is near a window. If Tobias has sent someone to photograph us, they will have a clear view. But scaling back the spectacle will be easy, everything except the flowers. Those have already been delivered and placed."

"But . . . are you absolutely sure a public proposal is necessary?" I croaked.

"It is necessary." He nodded at this statement. "Tobias will have someone there to observe from outside, certainly, but also likely a member of the waitstaff. It would be suspicious if I did not take the opportunity to move our relationship forward."

I inhaled a shaky breath, then reached for the box. I opened it. Inside was a simple, but beautiful and huge, square solitaire diamond set in a delicate platinum-colored band. It looked antique and expensive. Like, it could pay my rent for five years maybe.

"Is this real?" I croaked, peering up at him.

"Yes. The appraisal is in the safe of my apartment if you would like to see it."

"That won't be necessary." I tried to smile but wasn't sure I pulled it off. Closing the box, I placed it back on the seat between us and rubbed my forehead, speaking in a stream of consciousness. "Regarding the level of ostentatiousness, I think you should go with whatever you—as yourself—would typically do. If you put on a big show but you're not a showy person, it would look fake. Right?"

Andreas's eyes lost focus for a second, ostensibly in deliberation, then he nodded. "A fair point. I will tell the maître d' to scale it back to candlelight and champagne."

Ugh. That sounds so nice.

"And for the, um, PDA . . ." I found I had to exhale past the strange tightness in my chest and reaffix my eyes to the interior of the car—so, not Andreas—in order to approach this question with the appropriate amount of detachment.

You're a scientist, for God's sake. Be analytical!

Without giving it too much thought, I added, "We should hug and kiss for sure. If we don't, after a proposal, that would seem bizarre. And like, an actual kiss. Not a peck." I peeked at him. "Is that okay with you?"

He smiled, just a little. "I concur."

Oh. You concur, do you? Based on his tone of voice and his word usage, I suspected he didn't quite understand what I meant.

Facing him fully, I spoke to both him and myself as I said resolutely, "I'm serious. If there is one time we should go overboard with the PDA, it's tonight. Okay? So, gird your loins. I'll probably kiss your face off."

Andreas's smile seemed to flatten even as his lips twitched. "Noted."

"I'm trying to prepare you." I lifted my index finger and pointed at him. "Expect tongue. Lots of it. And my hands will be grabby. I'm a grabby kisser."

He gave me a single, slow blink.

But I wasn't finished. "I also bite."

All traces of his smile vanished.

"That's right, I'm a biter."

He faced forward and cleared his throat.

"And a licker. And—"

"I understand. No need to continue." He interrupted me, shifting in his seat, his tone flat.

"But—"

"Please stop."

"But—"

He held up a hand. "I consider myself duly prepared. I assure you, no further descriptions are required."

I was just about to push the issue when I noticed the car had slowed. Glancing out the window beyond Andreas, I realized Tara had pulled alongside the restaurant and I bit the inside of my bottom lip. The lights within—mostly candlelight—were golden and warm, and vases and baskets of red roses had been packed into the space. The interior appeared free of customers, but I spotted a few servers.

Andreas cleared his throat again, bringing my attention back to him. "Ready?"

It took me a second, but I nodded. "Yeah. I'm ready."

He opened the door, paused as though thinking, then turned back to me. "You should hold my hand, as you exit. Let me help you out."

I nodded, steeling myself for the feel of his hand in mine again. That decided, Andreas then fully exited the car and stood just outside, hand extended.

I hesitated, then accepted his fingers, ignoring the spike of warmth jolting up my arm, and let him lead me out onto the sidewalk. The air was cold, but I didn't feel it.

Silly me was already flushed, thinking ten steps ahead to the moment when I'd have to kiss him.

* * *

Andreas and I were deep into a passionate argument about which era of *Star Trek* movies was superior when the server, clearly not wanting to interrupt, hovered at the edge of the table like a shadow. I ignored him. I was on a roll.

"How can you argue with the whales?" I leaned forward, pressing my palm to the top of the table. "*Star Trek* four has the whales! And it takes place in the eighties. Oh! And! And! Time travel. Huh? Right? I'm right, right?" Crossing my arms, I nodded.

Andreas, who'd maintained the facial expression of an automaton —granted, a sexy, smoldering automaton—during most of our meetings since our renewed acquaintance was now actually showing signs of life tonight. His new repertoire of facial expressions this evening had been revelation: eyebrow flickering, a faint crease at the corners of his mouth, even a real smirk of amusement when I described *The Original Series* crew as "a fleet of accidental gay icons."

Presently, he also crossed his arms, dangerously close to a smile that would show teeth, and shook his head. "You can't tell me *Star Trek* four is better than the 2009 reboot."

I gasped, even though I already knew this was his position on the subject since he'd said so minutes ago. "It's like I don't even know you. Tell me the truth, were you taken over by the Zetar? Lieutenant Romaine, are you in there? Do you have Zetarian spirits inside you now?"

We'd already finished our main courses—mine, a fillet of perfectly rare steak with truffled brussels sprouts; his, a warm French lentil salad followed by a seitan bourguignon—and we were working our way through a bottle of Côtes du Rhône AOC rosé that I would never be able afford under any circumstances. But Andreas didn't seem to notice the prices.

Dessert was somewhere in our future. For now, our little round table was a battlefield of quips, pop-culture references, and the occasional flicker of what felt like dangerous chemistry.

If I were to provide an objective, scientific analysis of the evening thus far, I'd say it started stiff and mannered, with both of us trying to perform normally in front of an audience that, as far as I could tell, consisted solely of the manager, a friendly sommelier, and a rotating cast of waiters so discreet thus far, they might've been deployed by the CIA.

And then, about halfway through the first glass of wine, I'd asked Andreas whether he still built pillow forts. And just like that, the ice had cracked.

I'd forgotten how intensely he could focus when talking about something that mattered to him. It was honestly intoxicating. For a long time, I let him monologue about the internal politics of the chess tournaments, the way social media had commodified all the top players, and why he'd decided to stop allowing comments on his posts and photos after strange conspiracy theories and shipping wars broke out between his fandom and another grand master's.

That's right. Members of Andreas's legions of fans had started shipping him with another grand master, another nonfiction human. And, apparently, there were fanfics.

Mental note. Look those up later. For reasons.

His face, usually a monument to European stoicism, had become animated as he explained the different flavors of cheating, mostly having to do with vibration devices planted in shoes or—*ahem*—shoved up buttholes. This portion of our conversation had me laughing so hard, I'd almost snorted rosé out of my nose. Good times.

But the best part? He actually laughed. Not once, but twice. And each time it startled him so much he immediately tried to cover it up by taking a sip of wine or running a hand through his already-mussed hair or dipping his chin down. Watching him try to hold it together was maybe the best thing I'd experienced in months.

"Okay," I said, topping off my own glass and leaning across the table, "but if you had to choose: *Next Generation* or *Deep Space Nine*?"

Andreas's eyes narrowed in mock seriousness. "An unfair question. They are fundamentally different."

"Coward." I pretended to be disgusted. "Cop-out. You have to pick one. Gun to your head."

He considered this, his expression serious and unfocused, as though giving it intense deliberation. Abruptly, his eyes sharpened on me. "*Deep Space Nine.*"

I put a hand over my heart. "God, that's a power move. They're not even on a ship."

He grinned, the smile quick and real, like my praise pleased him immensely. Andreas opened his mouth, then shut it again, lips pressed together to hold back another smile. "You are," he said after a beat, "just as fun to be around as I remembered."

"Flattery will get you everywhere." I winked and drained the last of my wine.

We fell into a silence, not awkward, just comfortable. I glanced down and realized my hand was resting on the edge of the table, fingers curled in a way that practically begged to be held. It wasn't intentional, but it also wasn't not intentional. Andreas's hand—long fingers, knuckles like marble—lay close enough that if I reached just an inch or two, I could bridge the gap.

For a second, I considered moving my hand away, but then I remembered the rules. Rules which we'd drafted together and which stated quite clearly that hand holding was not only permitted, but expected.

Good thing he doesn't know about my hand kink.

Giving in, I reached over and put my hand on top of his, soft and casual, like it was no big deal. Like I'd done it a million times before.

He immediately turned his palm up, catching my fingers in a loose but inescapable hold. Then he pulled my hand closer, into the narrow space between our wineglasses, and for the next few moments, he absentmindedly traced circles on the back of my hand with his thumb while we debated the finer points of the time loop movies.

If I'd been a spectator, I would've bet money that we were very much in like—and lust—and not, as was actually the case, running a long con against a cabal of corporate sociopaths. I wanted to give myself a high five for my acting prowess. Except none of this felt like acting. It was just easy. Fun. Comfortable and exhilarating.

More than that, I thoroughly enjoyed trying to make Andreas lose his composure. Not just because it was a challenge—it absolutely was —but because every time he let his guard down, even a little, the world got about twenty percent less bleak and I felt, for a few precious seconds, like I wasn't just someone orbiting in his gravity well, but an equal. A true partner. Perhaps even a friend.

The waiter appeared with a miniature lake of vegan crème brûlée and set it between us, necessitating that we stop holding hands. *Alas.*

I picked up my spoon and broke the sugar-crust top. "Tell me something." I scooped out a spoonful, eyes on Andreas. "What's the dumbest thing you've ever done to impress a girl?"

Andreas set down the spoon he'd just picked up and studied me for a moment, the tiniest hint of a smile tugging at his lips. "This. Right now."

I made a noise, half laugh, half snort, and nearly inhaled a mouthful of burnt sugar. "You realize you're supposed to say something like, 'Bought a sports team' or 'Fought a bear.'"

"I have never fought a bear," he said, straight-faced.

"That's too bad," I replied. "Women love a bear fighter."

He laughed. It was a real one, low and gravelly and full-bodied, and I felt it like a jolt down my spine. Almost immediately, he tried to stifle it, shaking his head. "You are ridiculous."

I beamed at him, enjoying the victory. "Why do you do that? Why do you try to stop yourself from laughing?"

He blinked, caught off guard by the question. "I do not stop myself."

I raised an eyebrow. "You literally just did. Three times."

He looked away, as if the wall of Bordeaux bottles behind me could provide an answer. "I suppose I am not used to it."

"That's tragic," I said, shaking my head in mock sympathy. "You used to laugh all the time, back when we were kids."

Andreas picked up his wineglass, swirling the pink liquid before taking a measured sip. He seemed to really consider my statement, perhaps parsing it for subtext. When he finally answered, his voice was softer. "Maybe. I think I laugh now, too, just not . . ." He trailed off, maybe searching for how to best explain. "Just not with everyone."

"Just with people who are funny?"

Andreas nodded, not looking at me.

"Is this your way of saying I'm funny?"

He glanced up then, and for the first time all night, his expression seemed to open. His eyes moved over my face, then my neck, then the neckline of my dress, which—let's be honest—didn't leave a ton to the imagination.

"Very," he said, gaze sliding up from my chest to my neck, my lips, and eventually tangling with my eyes. "Among other things."

The words landed somewhere between my heart and my stomach and lit a little fuse. I had to fight a blush. Blushing was for people who didn't know better. Yet, the look he gave me, the directness of his stare and the obvious meaning behind his words, made my head spin a little.

He's a good actor.

As if on cue, a member of the waitstaff approached, moving with a careful, almost reverent gait.

"Is everything to your liking?" he asked Andreas, but his gaze flicked to me for a split second, as if checking for signs of distress.

Andreas never took his eyes from mine. "Yes," he said, voice low. "I believe we are ready."

The waiter gave a tiny, satisfied bow and retreated.

I placed both elbows on the table, chin in my palm, and regarded Andreas over the rim of my glass. "So," I said in a conspiratorial whisper, "is it happening now? Are you going to propose?"

He stared back at me with those mesmerizing green eyes and gave the tiniest nod.

I grinned even though this was a farce and we both knew it. But there was something thrilling about it, too. Like being on a rollercoaster you knew was perfectly safe. For a moment, I let myself imagine it was real and risky. That someone would actually propose to me, here, in this beautiful restaurant, and that I would say yes, and that we'd live a perfectly normal, boring life together, free of drama and academic warfare and corporate sabotage.

But then I remembered that the only thing I'd ever wanted less than academic warfare was marriage. If anyone ever proposed to me in real life, I'd probably change my phone number and move to a different state. And if I ever saw them walking down the street, I'd walk the other way.

Still. I understood why people did it. I understood the desire to be seen and known, to claim and be claimed, to say, "This is my person. This is the one I want forever."

But I also understood, maybe more than anyone, that nothing actually lasted forever. And I'd rather be alone and unbroken than risk loving someone so much it would eventually destroy me when they died, or left, or lost interest.

Andreas reached across the table and plucked my hand from

beneath my chin, holding it between both of his. His grip was warm and firm. I could see his jaw flex with tension, yet his touch was gentle.

He leaned forward, so only I could hear, and whispered, "Ready?"

I swallowed, my throat tight because this man used to be my best friend as a kid, and my first real crush as a preteen. And now he was going to fake propose to me and I was going to fake accept. How absurd was that?

I nodded anyway.

Andreas stood. He took a breath. He didn't look at anyone but me.

Then he got down on one knee.

My eyes widened and I felt a hush fall over the room, probably born of my own imagination. But I hadn't expected him to kneel. Not in a million years. I was supposed to be acting, but my surprise at his gesture was genuine.

Andreas, still kneeling, took the small velvet box he'd shown me in the car earlier from his pocket and opened it. The diamond sparkled and looked like a fantasy.

He gazed at me, features deadly serious, and said, "Samantha, I think I have loved you from the first moment I saw you. It is one of my earliest memories, branded in my mind and on my soul. You wore burgundy, like tonight, and pigtails, and I recall thinking you were the most amazing, brilliant, interesting, fascinating person in the world, and every moment spent with you since has only reinforced this belief. I cannot believe I am lucky enough to ask you this question."

Heat erupted in my chest and stinging liquid emotion rushed to my eyes. I found I had to blink to keep Andreas in focus.

He paused, only for a second, then asked, "Will you marry me?"

The room was silent. I felt eyes on us. And then I did the stupidest thing I'd done in a decade. I started crying real tears.

It wasn't a sob, not at first. My chin wobbled. One single, traitorous drop rolled down my face. I tried to laugh it off, but the laugh cracked and shattered and became a gasp.

Andreas's face, usually so unreadable, changed. He stared at me, visibly uncertain, his lips parted. There was a flash of alarm, and I realized he was afraid he'd upset me, even though this was all a game.

I forced myself to nod, once, then again, harder, so everyone in the room could see.

"Yes," I said, voice barely a whisper.

Exhaling like he'd been worried I might say no, Andreas stood, slipped the ring onto my finger, and before I could think about it, I also stood and threw my arms around his neck. I hugged him with everything I had. He hugged me back, tight and close, like he meant it. And for a second, my cheek pressed against his neck, I let myself believe he did.

The room erupted in applause, presumably from the waitstaff, and I tangentially wondered if they'd been paid to clap.

Pulling back, I'm sure tears streaked my makeup. Andreas caught my face in both hands, cradling my cheeks. There was a moment of silent negotiation. *Should we kiss now*? his eyes seemed to ask.

We had to, obviously. It was expected. It was required.

Andreas leaned in. I closed my eyes. Our lips met. And this first kiss was nothing like I'd imagined it would be when we'd discussed it in the car.

I'd expected his part to be cold, calculated pressure, a kind of mechanical lip touch that was only technically a kiss. Instead, his lips were soft, lingering, warm. He kissed me slowly, like he was savoring me, and for a second the world went fuzzy at the edges. My heart slammed against my ribs so hard I thought it might bruise, and I felt my body melt into him. When he eventually pulled back, I was legitimately dizzy, and I was certain my face was flushed, and I had only one thought in my head.

Jesus fucking Christ, he has amazing lips.

Something greedy and reckless took hold of me. I grabbed the lapels of his suit and pulled him closer, intent not just on playing my role but on giving myself something I'd never forget. I wanted him, to know if the memory of his mouth would match the daydreams of my youth. My lips crashed into his, not gentle or tentative, but decisive, demanding. I pressed into him, feeling the solid, unyielding line of his chest through my dress, and let my tongue trace along the seam of his lips.

For half a beat he tensed, as if surprised by my boldness, then surrendered without hesitation. But then, I'd warned him there'd be tongue. Hadn't I?

His lips parted and I pushed inside, the heat of him igniting something ferocious within me. Andreas made a low, involuntary sound—somewhere between a moan and a gasp—a tiny, startled noise, the kind I'd only ever heard in moments of genuine surprise. The fact that I'd ripped it out of him made adrenaline zing down my spine and I pushed for more.

He responded in kind. His hands, previously gentle and scripted for the crowd of restaurant staff, clamped onto my lower back with purpose. His grip was solid, fingers digging into the silk of my dress and hips, pulling me flush against him until there was nothing between us, no room for anything but the incendiary heat of our bodies. In that moment, I was hyper-aware of the way his forearm flexed along my side, the hard tremor of his ribs against my own, even the delicate scent of the cologne he wore, now mingled with the citrusy tang of wine.

This second kiss was so much wetter, so much noisier, so much more ravenous. My hands climbed to the nape of his neck, threading through the soft hair, and I felt the shiver run all the way through him. I was distantly aware of movement in the background, a clink of glasses and the hum of waitstaff blurred together. But the only thing that really existed was the hot slide of his tongue against mine and the pressure of his body pinning me to the moment.

He broke away just enough to catch his breath, but when he tried to pull back, I chased him, biting at his lower lip. I felt him smile, felt his teeth graze my own, and that was enough to make me laugh out loud, giddy and breathless. He swallowed the laugh, mouth returning for another kiss, and this time he took control, grabbing my hair and angling my head back with a yank so he could kiss me deeper. I let him, because I wanted it—I wanted it so badly my pulse was thrumming in places I'd been neglecting for years. His tongue flicked against my own and my whole body lit up with goose bumps. I heard myself make a soft, desperate noise, and I would have been embarrassed if I'd had the capacity for shame.

His hands moved, one splayed across my back while the other cupped my jaw, thumb stroking down my neck, hot palm sliding to my shoulder, fingers playing with the strap of my dress. I opened my eyes for a second, saw his were still closed, and suddenly I was terrified, because for an instant I wasn't sure if he was still acting or if this was real, if he could possibly be feeling even a fraction of what was detonating inside me.

That thought had me pulling away, my lungs burning, and I blinked at him. He stared back, pupils blown so wide, his eyes looked almost black. His lips were swollen, his face flushed with heat, and for a flicker of a second, I thought he was going to say something, actually say something real, but instead he just yanked me forward, quick and sharp, and kissed me again. I felt the ring on my finger press against his cheek.

I couldn't have said how long we stood there, locked together in the center of that restaurant, kissing each other. For all I knew, we had stopped time itself. I slid my hands down from his hair, traced his jaw with my thumbs, tried to memorize every detail of this moment because I knew it wouldn't happen again.

It is a special circumstance, he'd said.

Which meant, this was it. This was my one and only chance to kiss him. He'd agreed in the car. This was allowed.

And, worse, this was the best kiss of my life *by far*, a fact that was so dismaying I almost laughed just to keep from crying. Because I'd promised myself I'd never let anyone get under my skin like this, never allow myself to get carried away.

But hadn't Andreas Kristiansen always been the exception? He'd been grandfathered in, before my life had gone to hell, and I'd cared about him so deeply before I understood the potential danger, before I—

Abruptly, there was a loud *pop*. We flinched apart, Andreas's hands still locked on my back. I blinked at my surroundings, spotting the waiter and the sommelier from before standing nearby, holding a silver bucket with an open bottle of champagne. The friendly sommelier was smiling, the waiter trying desperately not to.

Mercifully, Andreas let me go, just enough to turn and face the onlookers. He slid his hand down my arm, threading his fingers through mine, and I let him. I also let him kiss my hand, soft and old-fashioned. For a second, I fought the desperate desire to pull him back in for another round.

I had to remind myself why we were here, what this entire spectacle was really about. With this reminder, the world snapped back into focus. I glanced past the sommelier, scanning the room for anyone who seemed out of place, anyone who might be watching for Tobias or Henrik, and spotted a waitress behind the manager slipping her phone back into her pocket, her eyes shifty.

Mission accomplished . . . *I guess.*

Meanwhile, Andreas's thumb slid over my knuckles, slow and deliberate, and the sensation was so intimate I almost forgot my own name. I let myself lean into him one last time, pressing my cheek against his shoulder, breathing him in. He rested his chin lightly on my head, and I said goodbye to the fantasy. Mourned it. Because out-of-control longing wasn't for me.

But it had been lovely to pretend, if only for a little while.

The waitstaff descended upon us with congratulations, the bottle of champagne, and two flutes already filled to the brim. The manager offered her own best wishes, beaming at us as if she'd played a role in our engagement. I tried to smile, to play along, but I felt hollowed out, like a building gutted by fire. I didn't dare look at Andreas for fear of what I'd see there.

Or what I might show him in return.

[13]
DNA TECHNOLOGY

Samantha

Thirty-one minutes after accepting a fake marriage proposal, I sat in the back of the Mercedes SUV staring holes through the seat in front of me. The privacy window was down and Tara drove with both hands on the wheel, posture immaculate. I sat directly behind her and the middle seat between me and Andreas was left vacant. Andreas, whose own back was pressed flat to the leather, kept his gaze fixed out the window as the city blurred past in electric streaks. He hadn't said a word since we'd left the restaurant. He also hadn't touched me, not even an accidental graze.

I kept waiting for some kind of follow-up. A postmortem of the proposal. A joke. Instead, the only reminder of the whole spectacle was the diamond on my finger, a sparkling star that winked whenever I turned my hand. I still wasn't convinced it wasn't a prop, the weight of it felt obscene.

The proposal, the champagne, the public make out so hot it still echoed beneath my skin, all of it played on a loop during brittle quiet of the car ride. For reasons I couldn't name, I felt like crying. It wasn't sadness, more like sheer *overwhelm*, the way one might cry after narrowly avoiding being hit by a bus.

Tara checked on me in the mirror, watching me with open curiosity. I attempted a smile, but it died halfway up my cheeks.

She caught it anyway. Her own smile flashed, then vanished as quickly as it came.

Andreas was the first to speak, his voice smooth and impassive. "Do you want the movers to come tomorrow, or Sunday?"

I flinched slightly at the sudden sound. "Um, tomorrow's fine," I said, and forced myself to unclench my jaw. "I should be finished packing before noon."

"Do you need boxes?" His eyes were still pointed out the window.

I shook my head even though he wasn't looking at me. "No. I have stackable bins for moving. I've done it so many times that I just keep them in my closet. It'll be four bins and a suitcase. The furniture stays."

At this, Andreas faced me wearing a confused-looking frown. He studied me for a long moment, like he had several follow-up questions. But eventually, the tiny crease that had formed above his nose smoothed, and he redirected his gaze out the window again. "I will tell them to come at noon, then."

That was it. No further conversation. Tara, perhaps sensing the silence had crystallized, turned on a playlist that apparently consisted of only cello covers of pop songs. "Wrecking Ball" had never sounded so apt.

The car ate the blocks between Midtown and the far side of the park. I counted every stoplight, every jogger, every office worker fumbling with their phone late on a Friday night. I wondered what they'd think if they looked through the tinted glass and saw me, diamond ring on my left hand, hair still flawless, makeup less so, and dead-eyed with the particular numbness that follows a massive adrenaline spike.

Maybe they'd think I was some trophy wife on the way home from a charity ball. Or maybe they'd see what was really going on, a girl who'd just sold her soul for a shot at poetic justice, and now had to pretend like the consequences weren't already gnawing at her.

When we pulled up to my building, Tara put the car in park and looked over her shoulder. "Do you want me to wait?"

I'd already started to reach for the door, but Andreas caught my wrist before I could open it. The contact startled me, not because it was rough, but because it was so careful.

"I will walk Samantha up to her apartment." His words sounded coldly polite. "Please circle the block until I return."

Tara gave a little salute. "Sure thing, boss."

Andreas exited first, walked around the back of the car, and opened my door for me. He offered his hand. I took it and our fingers fit together. His was a little clammy, and mine was probably freezing. I let him lead me to the door and studied his posture as we walked. He appeared entirely at ease, his movements unhurried.

At the front entrance, I typed in the security code. He didn't let go of my hand as the door buzzed open and we crossed the threshold.

Inside, the stairwell was dim and quiet, the scent of old radiators and paint chips mixing with the faintest whiff of the bakery down the block. I paused, at a loss for what to do next.

Andreas finally released my hand, stuffing both of his into his coat pockets. He looked up the stairs, seeming to contemplate each one individually, like the act of walking me up to my apartment was perhaps the most complicated situation he'd ever encountered.

I shifted my weight, fished through my bag for keys I didn't quite need yet, gave up searching for them, and tried to think of something casual to say. "You know, it's four flights. You really don't have to walk me all the way up."

"I do not mind."

"It's not dangerous," I pressed, feigning exasperation I didn't feel. "I don't need an escort. Honestly, it's fine. I'll just go up from here."

I wanted him to leave. Not because I didn't want him around, but because the moment he left, I could finally collapse and let the tears— tears I didn't understand and didn't want to explain—have their way with me. Diya should be at work unless something in her schedule had changed last minute. Kendra was at her boyfriend's. And Nakita had left this afternoon for her parents' place outside of Boston. I'd have the whole apartment to myself.

But Andreas didn't leave. He looked at the stairs, then at his shoes, then back at me. "I need to wait here for fifteen minutes."

That threw me. "Why?"

"It would be strange"—his gaze locked on a spot above my head—"for me to sleep alone tonight after that proposal."

It took a few seconds for the logic to sink in. Then it hit all at once. He was performing for an audience we knew existed, and was watching, and was likely outside the building. One I'd already forgotten about in my post-kiss haze. If anyone had followed us to my building —likely one of Tobias's underlings—they'd expect Andreas to spend the night.

I felt a laugh rise in my chest, but it came out bitter. "Right. Of course."

And then, because my brain always insisted on poking holes in plans, I asked, "What if they spot you leaving after fifteen minutes? Won't that look suspicious?"

He cleared his throat, but didn't answer. For once, the strategic genius had no ready move. I could almost see the gears grinding behind his stoic mask.

I took a step up, then stopped and turned, arms folded. "Should you just spend the night, then?"

His eyes snapped to mine. If I hadn't been staring, I might have missed the way they widened, just for a second, with what looked like astonishment.

"Do you want me to spend the night?" The question hung between us, utterly flat and uninflected.

I opened my mouth, then closed it. Thoughts tumbled in. The taste of his mouth, the smell of rosemary, the way his hand had fit against the small of my back and made me feel like my bones were electric. I remembered, too, the rules. No physical contact when alone. No room for the real thing.

I shrugged, hoping it looked cool and unbothered. "If there's a chance you'll be spotted leaving and it messes up our plan, then yes. I'll text Diya and see if she's coming home tonight. If not, you can have my bed, I'll take hers. Otherwise, you can sleep on the couch."

Andreas's eyebrows pulled together in not quite a frown. "Is that what you want?"

I should have said, *It doesn't matter what I want. The plan is all that matters.* But the thought of him in my apartment, of waking up and seeing him there, even as an act, sent a pulse of longing through me that was so strong I wanted to kick myself.

"It's fine," I said tiredly, and started up the stairs. "Whatever makes sense." I paused, thumb hovering over my phone, and shot Diya a text.

Sam: Home early. You have an overnight shift, right? Need to know for . . . reasons.

While waiting for her reply, I continued climbing stairs. I'd ascended two flights before I noticed I was climbing them alone. I stopped, turned, and looked down. Andreas was a full flight below me, face angled up, standing motionless on the landing.

He wasn't winded. In fact, he looked like a malfunctioning Roomba, immobilized by indecision, calculating alternate routes. His face was marble, unreadable except for the barest tightness in the line of his jaw.

"You okay?" I asked, pitching my voice as low as I could, wanting to irritate my neighbors as little as possible.

His gaze shifted to mine and he nodded once. Then he started up the stairs, climbing in a steady, silent cadence until he reached my level.

We walked the rest of the way together, no more than a step apart, neither of us speaking. My thoughts scurried in a dozen directions. Why had he stopped? Did I do something wrong? Was he regretting the whole public display at the restaurant? Had I bitten him too hard during the kiss? Did he realize, suddenly, that he would have to sleep on my sad, lumpy mattress and was recalculating the entire trajectory of his life up to this moment?

I checked my phone at the landing. Diya hadn't replied to my earlier text, so I fired off another.

Sam: Hey, if you won't be home tonight, is it cool if Andreas stays over? I'll sleep in your bed, he'll sleep in mine. LMK if you're coming home tonight.

I sent it, then fumbled for my keys. Andreas reached out—quick, efficient—and took my clutch before I could drop it. Then he held it open so I could use both my hands to find my keys. For some reason, this tiny, proactive gesture sent a shock wave of embarrassment down my spine.

He was so . . . thoughtful.

Muttering thanks once I'd found my keys, I moved to the locks. He followed me to the door, standing close enough for me to catch the faint hint of cologne beneath the more assertive scent of his rosemary shampoo.

I unlocked the top dead bolt, then the middle one, then the bottom, aware that each click ricocheted and echoed down the hallway.

Pushing open the door, I stepped inside. "Why don't you—"

Nakita's voice rang out, surprising and interrupting me. "Who's home? I'm in the kitchen. Don't be alarmed by the smoke." Her inflection was cheerful, so I assumed the smoke coming from the kitchen was purposeful.

But I stiffened, because she wasn't supposed to be home, which meant I half hollered, half screeched, "What are you doing here?! Aren't you supposed to be in Boston?"

Shit. I hadn't excepted anyone. And of my roommates, Nakita was the one I wanted to see the least right now considering she was the hardcore chess fangirl.

"Sam?"

I looked at Andreas's face; he wore his usual unemotional mask as I called back in a more modulated tone, "Yes. It's Sam, and—"

"Oh my God, Sam!" Nakita bellowed. "I have a bone to pick with you. I can't believe you actually know Andreas Kristiansen! Why wouldn't you tell me that you know the sexiest man in the world?"

Andreas stood perfectly still, holding my bag in one hand. Meanwhile, I cringed. With my whole body.

That's right. *A WHOLE-BODY CRINGE.*

Nakita continued, "That man can fill out a pair of pants, am I right? So hot. And don't even get me started on his chest and hands. Jesus Christ, I didn't expect him to be so tall! I wanted to climb him. Please tell me you're going to hit that—"

Belatedly finding my voice, I cut her off, loud and frantic. "He's standing right next to me, Nakita!"

Dead silence.

I peeked at Andreas again. His features hadn't changed, but there was a suggestion—just a suggestion—of mortification in the way he kept his eyes glued forward. For Andreas, and what I was coming to understand about his lack of external expressiveness, this felt like a big reaction.

Andreas had been a bit arrogant about his chess abilities the last time he was here, but Nakita's objectification now seemed to distress him greatly.

Is this modesty?

He had to know how handsome he was. How could he not?

Modest about his looks but arrogant about chess.

I unwrapped my scarf from my suddenly hot neck, whispering, "Sorry. I'm sorry. Are you okay? Do you want to leave?"

Andreas shook his head wordlessly, issuing me an exceedingly small, tight smile, and set my bag down on the entry table. I studied him as he shrugged off his coat, folding it over one arm with slow, precise movements.

"Andreas." I stepped closer, my voice just above a whisper while I barely resisted the urge to place a hand on his forearm. "We can go. I didn't know anyone would be here tonight. We can—"

He shook his head again, a calculating gleam entering his eyes. "No. This might be for the best."

I stared at him. "Uh, how so?"

Before he could respond, Nakita's quick footsteps interrupted our whispered conversation. She rounded the corner, her hands ensconced in oven mitts, the perfect portrait of domestic instability. Her cheeks were flushed, her braids pulled back into a haphazard bun, and her eyes were wide with apology.

"Oh. Hey, Andreas. I, uh, didn't know you were here." The words tripped over each other, and she sounded completely mortified. Gaze wide with obvious worry, she blurted, "I am so, so sorry. That was gross and rude and uncalled for and I'm sorry."

Saying nothing, Andreas lifted his chin in acknowledgment. Thankfully, he looked slightly less embarrassed than he had a second ago. Nakita turned to me, her eyes screaming *HELP*, and I mentally sent her a sympathy card. But also, she needed to learn: Don't say anything behind a person's back that you wouldn't say to their face. Ever.

Think that kind of shit to your heart's content, but don't say it.

"Where is the bathroom?" Andreas asked, voice low, attention sliding to me.

"Down the hall, first door before my bedroom. Leave your coat on my bed if you want." I lifted my chin in the direction of my room.

He nodded, then sedately strolled away, eventually vanishing behind the door of the restroom, which closed with an unhurried, soft *snick*.

The instant the door closed, Nakita whirled on me. "Oh my God, I'm so embarrassed. Why didn't you say he was here? I sounded like a total idiot. I literally called him the sexiest man in the world." She smacked her lips with her oven-mitt-clad fingers. "I'm so stupid."

Her embarrassment and worry cracked through my cloak of numbness and suddenly I was fighting a laugh at her discomfort. "You apologized. And he probably gets it a lot from people who don't apologize."

"No," Nakita said, shaking her head, "nobody gets that a lot. People don't just casually say that kind of thing in real life. Or they shouldn't. Oh my God. Please tell him I'm not a gross lecher."

I patted her arm, letting the contact linger. "You're not a gross lecher. You're just . . . aggressively fangirly and inappropriate."

Nakita gave me a wincing smile, then, with the finely honed skill of a lifelong gossip, scanned me from head to toe. "Speaking of sexy, what are you wearing? Holy hot sauce, Sam. You look incredible."

I looked down at myself. The dress still clung to me, the color now more dark-pool-of-blood than burgundy in the dim entryway. My heels felt less "elegant" and more "torture device" with every passing minute, but I tried to stand up straighter.

"It's a nice dress, right?" I said, voice tight, glancing toward the bathroom and wondering what to do if Nakita asked again about what was going on between Andreas and me.

You'll lie, of course, and tell her you're engaged. My stomach tried to sink. I wouldn't let it. Lying to my roommates would likely be the least of my deceptions over the coming months. I needed to get used to feeling icky.

"It's more than nice. Is that what you wore to dinner with him? Please tell me you just got back from a date, because both of you look like you stepped off a catwalk." Nakita took a step back and clasped her oven-mitted hands together. "And his suit matched!"

The weight of the ring on my finger became a black hole, compressing every nerve ending in my hand into a singularity. I thought about hiding it, then decided hiding it would only make things worse later. Better to get this over with.

I took a deep breath. "Actually, there's something I should tell you."

Nakita leaned in, eyes bright, hungry for gossip. And, boy oh boy, did I have a whole damn seven-course meal to feed her. She was about to get heartburn.

Seeing no reason to delay, I held up my left hand, ring finger exposed. "We're engaged."

Her mouth fell open, her eyes bugged out, and for a long moment she stared at me wordlessly.

Again, I actively worked to feel okay about lying. Strangely, I didn't have to try very hard. *Huh.*

"Engaged?" she finally squealed. "You're engaged?!"

I nodded, pasting on a large smile. I didn't feel like nodding or smiling, but I also didn't feel like I had any other available options. That said, the lie didn't even taste like a lie. It tasted oddly sweet, like the first sinister step toward my revenge.

* * *

After my reveal, Nakita worked her way through the five stages of gossip grief. She started with denial ("You're messing with me. No way you're engaged. Is this a prank? I'm not falling for it, Sam."), then anger ("This is so unfair, I tell you everything and you hold out on me like it's a state secret!"), then bargaining ("If you make me a bridesmaid, I'll plan your bachelorette party."), then depression ("Am I going to lose you? Are you going to move to Europe? Will you even visit?"), and finally, acceptance ("Fine, I don't need to be a bridesmaid. But I'd like an invitation.").

What made this progression truly remarkable was that it all took place in the two minutes before Andreas exited the bathroom.

Now the three of us were sitting in the family room, Andreas and me on the couch, Nakita in the armchair. She seemed to be attempting banal chitchat, and I wondered if the only thing keeping her from a full-scale inquisition was her earlier foot-in-mouth moment. That, or the fact that Andreas and I, after sitting next to each other on the couch for a solid five minutes, had yet to make any physical contact. Not a single graze of fingers, not a foot nudged, not even a moment of mutual eye contact.

We probably looked, in a word, estranged.

Nakita must've noticed, of course. She noticed everything. The more we failed to act "engaged," the deeper her frown lines became.

My palms were sweating. This was not how a newly engaged couple was supposed to act. And since Nakita was the gossip in our group, she'd definitely tell everyone about our odd behavior.

Looking between us, she leaned forward, elbows on knees. "So, how did you propose? Sam's never told us anything about your relationship. I want all the details."

I opened my mouth, but Andreas beat me to it. "At Maison Lavande, after dinner." He shrugged, voice even. Understated, but entirely believable. "I am not very original."

Nakita's eyes doubled in size. "Are you kidding? Maison Lavande is legendary! That's so romantic. Sam, did you cry?"

I didn't have to fake the blush. "A little. It was a surprise."

"She cried," Andreas confirmed, tone so dry it could have desiccated a houseplant.

Nakita's frown intensified and her gaze shifted between us, full of suspicion. Apparently recovered from her earlier embarrassment, she asked, "Did you two get in a fight already? Is it about Sam's propensity for sleepwalking?" The question was obviously asked as a joke, but her eyes were sharp.

"Samantha sleepwalks?" Andreas's question sounded so earnest and innocent.

Before I could respond, Nakita's stare sharpened. "You didn't know?"

"It's no big deal." I shrugged, avoiding both Nakita's and Andreas's gazes. "Just once or twice. Probably because of stress at work." I felt Andreas's continued attention on my profile.

Damn it.

Something had to be done. I wasn't certain what, or how to clear it with Andreas before doing it. There'd been a shift since that kiss in the restaurant, a new hyper-awareness—at least on my side. Now, I couldn't bring myself to initiate contact with him again.

So, I did what any rational, fully grown adult plotting revenge would do: I devised a plan.

Step one: Get Nakita out of the living room, even if just for a few minutes.

Step two: Have a whispered strategy session with Andreas so we could agree on a baseline level of "believable PDA" for this situation.

Step three: Behave as a credible couple by the time Nakita returned.

It was a solid plan.

Now, what excuse can I give for our present awkwardness and what will get her to leave the room . . . ?

"Uh, so." I scratched my neck and did a passable job of looking self-deprecatingly embarrassed. "We came here sorta last minute without a plan. I know I didn't clear it with anyone first, sorry about that."

Her gaze moved between us. "Oh, that's fine. Don't worry about that."

I leaned forward, my voice dropping to a conspiratorial whisper. "To be honest, I told Andreas no one would be home."

Nakita blinked and I was pleased to see a light of understanding in her eyes. "Oh, so you two thought you'd have the place to your—"

"Sorry, that was inconsiderate of me. But since we're here"—I put my hand on Andreas's knee without looking at him and felt his thigh muscle flex at the contact—"do you mind if we stay?"

"Not at all!" Her attention flickered to where my hand sat on his leg then back to me. "Sorry if I ruined your plans."

I waved her apology away. "Are you kidding? I'm the one in the wrong here. But, the thing is, for Andreas to spend the night, I need pajamas for him. Do you think Kendra's boyfriend—"

"Kendra has some of her boyfriend's clothes in her bottom drawer," she said, jumping up. "He's about the same size as Andreas, right? Tall, but, like, not gym tall?"

"Yeah, I think so." I stood too, twisting my fingers. "Do you think she has anything?"

"Sure! I'll grab a pair of sweatpants and a T-shirt. Is that okay?" Nakita was already backing up toward the bedroom she shared with Kendra.

"That should work, if you're sure—"

She disappeared down the hall, her voice calling back, "I'm sure! And I'll be right back. Don't go anywhere!"

I plopped down on the sofa again and inspected Andreas. He didn't look comfortable, but he also didn't look uncomfortable. How did he do that?

Leaning in, I whispered harshly, "We're not acting very engaged right now."

Andreas sliced me a glare so sharp it could've cut a watermelon in half. "What do you want me to do?" he hissed through his teeth. "We have not yet discussed what PDA would be appropriate for this situation, and your conditions state—"

I leaned closer, my nose almost bumping his. "Obviously, we're going to have to improvise!"

His jaw flexed, and he said, low and tight, "I do not know where I am allowed to touch you."

My brain ran through all the possible answers and hurriedly settled on the only one that wouldn't lead to a lengthy negotiation.

"Touch me anywhere you want, okay? Just make it look real. Nakita is already suspicious, and if we want her to—"

The sound of footsteps cut me off, and before I even realized what was happening, Andreas reached over, grabbed my arm, and hauled me across the couch. In one fluid, dizzying motion, he maneuvered me into his lap, spun me to face him, and anchored my hips down with an ironclad grip.

Suddenly, I was straddling Andreas Kristiansen on my own living room sofa, my knees on either side of his thighs, my hands braced against his shoulders, not a single second to spare a thought for how indecently high this position had pushed my dress up.

I froze. We both froze, gazes clashing. Then, his hands—one on my thigh, the other at the nape of my neck—pulled me forward.

He kissed me.

Not a peck. Not a gentle brush of lips. A full-on, open-mouthed, hungry, wet, and breathtaking kiss. His tongue sweeping inside me with a confidence that brooked no hesitation. I didn't even tense for a nanosecond, instead immediately melting against him like a heat-activated polymer.

My arms wound around his neck, and my fingers tunneled into his hair. I could feel him, between my spread legs, growing harder and longer, and my heartbeat jackhammered against my chest, which, incidentally, was now pressed flush to his. I wondered if he could feel me, too. The tightness of my nipples and the wet heat between my legs just as obvious as his erection pressing into me.

Don't do it. Don't grind down. Don't. Don't. Don't—

I did and it felt so fucking good, essential. Andreas groaned, the sound a rumble reverberating from his chest to mine, his hand at my neck gripping harder. The kiss was so hot, so electric, that it must've fried every synapse in my brain. All the rules and boundaries and self-imposed restrictions evaporated. The only thing that existed was the urgency of his mouth on mine and the strong, commanding grip of his hands on my thigh and neck, and how much my body needed—

"Oh! Yikes! Gosh, sorry!"

At the sound of Nakita's reentrance, Andreas pulled away slightly and dipped his chin to break the kiss. He pressed his forehead against mine and we shared a few ragged breaths before he swallowed, leaned to the side, and looked—or rather, glared—at Nakita.

"Pardon. We will move this elsewhere."

[14]
BIOCHEMISTRY AND THE MOLECULES OF LIFE

Samantha

Wrapping an arm around my upper body and standing, Andreas didn't give my brain a chance to catch up with his intentions. Torso supported, my legs gradually slid from his hips to his calves until he bent slightly at the waist, setting my feet gently on the floor. I was about to untangle my arms from his neck when he leaned to my ear and whispered, "Hold on."

The heat of his breath falling against my bare skin made me shiver, but I complied, holding him tighter. Placing one arm under my legs, he scooped me up. Unsure what I was thinking or feeling, I buried my head in the crook of his neck and squeezed my eyes shut, focusing only on regulating my breathing and battling this overwhelming, drug-like daze of arousal.

I heard him murmur, "Thank you."

Andreas then carried me around the couch and down the short hallway to my room. I sensed him pause inside. He shifted. I heard the door close.

I felt his chest rise and fall with a sigh. "Are you alright?"

I nodded, my arms loosening. "Can you put me down, please?" My voice sounded odd, rough, small.

He bent and it didn't occur to me until he set me down that, due to the shortness of my hiked-up dress and the method of his transport—one-armed bridal-style carry—I'd likely just flashed Nakita.

Oh well. She can thank me for the free show later.

Rolling my eyes at myself, I felt my face go red, not because I'd flashed my roommate but because I'd been too turned on to notice. In a scramble to preserve any shred of dignity, I spent a frantic few seconds yanking my skirt down while stumbling away from Andreas, trying to remember what decorum even was.

Decorum. *What is: A word my grandmother used that I never learned, for $500, Alex?*

Still blushing so hard I thought my face might combust, I turned stupidly in a half circle, desperately wanting to fill the tense silence. "So, uh, you'll take—you'll sleep there." I pointed to my bed. "I should change the sheets."

"No need." Andreas walked toward my mattress and, in the dim illumination provided by the city lights coming in through the window, I realized he held a bundle of clothes. He lifted a pair of sweatpants. "These should fit."

Kendra's boyfriend's clothes. Andreas had likely one-arm carried me so he could accept the pajamas from Nakita without letting me go.

I did my level best to pretend the last ten minutes hadn't affected me by clearing my throat and attempting a nonchalant nod. "Good. And if you're cool with the sheets, fine. They were washed recently anyway." The effect was spoiled by the fact that my fingers visibly shook when I darted past him and fumbled with the light switch by the door. "I'll just—I'll go brush my—"

He was next to me in a flash, his larger hand covering mine on the switch. "Wait."

I went statue still, a now familiar jolt of electricity shooting up my arm at his touch.

"Don't. Your roommate is out there, and it would appear strange if you turned on the lights or left now, after . . ."

I made a short sound of agreement, like an ahh, and removed my fingers from the light switch.

A long, awkward moment passed where neither of us moved or spoke. My ears strained to listen for movement beyond the room, but the sound of my own heart beating between my temples made that impossible. And I was too turned on. Rather than allow my breathing to grow shallow or labored again, I held air in my lungs then forced myself to exhale carefully, slowly, silently through my nose.

"Samantha," he whispered roughly, breaking the silence, still standing too close but not touching me anywhere. "Are you . . . upset with me?"

"No," I croaked, then cleared my throat again before adding on a whisper, "Not at all. Are you upset with me?"

Daring to glance over my shoulder, I peeked at him. His back was to the window, his features were mostly in shadow, but I felt his eyes on me.

Finally, after a protracted period, he rasped out, "Not upset, no."

Those words sounded like a riddle. Instinctively, I turned, lifting my chin and searching his face, or what I could see of his features, which wasn't much. But his eyes seemed to glint.

It was on the tip of my tongue to ask what he'd meant when Andreas stumbled a step forward, as though he'd been pushed from behind. His hands reached out and gripped my waist, tugging me forward. His fingers flexed on my sides. The movement felt restless. I heard him exhale a ragged breath as his forehead connected with mine.

"I need—" he began, then shook his head, his arms abruptly embracing me. "May I hold you? I only need—only for a moment."

My arms were already returning his embrace before he'd finished speaking, wrapping tightly around his chest. I felt his erection against my stomach, hard and insistent, but I ignored it, and a long exhale left my lungs. Holding him right now felt necessary, a relief, an outlet for the buzzing electric energy beneath my skin. I closed my eyes, squeezing him tighter.

Ear pressed against his wide chest, I listened as his racing heart gradually slowed and our breathing synced. Eventually, I felt him swallow. He lifted a hand and gently pressed his palm to the crown of my head, as though encouraging me to snuggle closer, to relax into him. My arms loosened but I kept my fingers locked as I melted against his body, sinking into the warm strength of his arms.

We stood there so much longer than a moment, holding each other in the dim light. I didn't know what he was thinking and I made no effort to guess. Abruptly aware of how exposed I felt, both physically and otherwise, I knew I was being ridiculous and I needed to get my head on straight.

The sound of Nakita's bedroom door closing is what finally broke us apart.

I stepped away. He let me go. Then I turned my back to him and stared at my dresser, at the pile of unfolded laundry, at my poster of Rosalind Franklin glaring at me from the shadows with supreme judgment.

"If you're going to stay, you should change clothes." I moved further away from him. "I'll go get you a new toothbrush and lay it out in the bathroom. Let me give you some privacy," I said, a little too fast, a little too loud. I then grabbed my own pajamas from the drawer, bolted out the door, and shut it behind me.

Making a beeline for the bathroom, I ignored the sound of Nakita's laughter echoing from behind her closed bedroom door. Once inside, I turned the lock, found a new toothbrush, set it on the sink, and stared at myself in the mirror.

Somehow, my makeup had mostly survived the double onslaught of tears and tongue. My mascara was only slightly smeared, and my lipstick, while gone, had left behind a faint berry stain.

A laugh bubbled up, but it came out as something brittle and desperate.

I stripped out of the dress and shimmied into my pajamas—baggy, blue, and covered in cartoon mitochondria—then sat down on the edge of the bathtub, buried my face in my hands, and tried to process the events of the evening.

We'd had a *really* nice dinner together. In fact, if tonight's dinner had been a real first date, it would've been the best one I'd ever had. And then everything that came after . . .

This was dangerous. This was uncharted territory. I was the one who'd insisted on boundaries, on rules, on avoiding any scenario where I might get in over my head. And now, I was the one who couldn't get her heart rate below 160.

I needed to talk to Andreas, be honest, and put it all out there. I needed to clarify. To define. To make sure that what happened in the restaurant and on the sofa were simply one-time-only—er, two-time-only—mission-critical incidents, and not gateway grope fests that would lead to . . . something else.

But first, I needed a few more minutes alone.

Pressing my palms to my eyelids, I attempted to memorize the feeling of his hands on my hips, his mouth on mine, the dizzying, impossible heat of his body beneath my open legs. I tried to memorize it so I could lock it away forever, file it under "Miscellaneous," and get on with the task at hand: burning it all down and coming out the other side unscathed and triumphant.

Unfortunately, there was also the small matter of *the hug* in my bedroom just now. Unscripted, unnecessary, and very private. Some part of me had desperately craved that embrace from Andreas, and had been craving it since he first approached me outside my department building. All this strange wistfulness I'd been trying to shove aside and ignore, longing I'd labeled as simple attraction, when my feelings were so much deeper than surface-level desire.

But, so what? What could be done about it? Sure, I'd have to confront it, talk it out, establish new boundaries, especially since we'd be moving in together tomorrow. But I could never allow myself to act on this wistfulness and longing. Too much was at stake.

I had a fake fiancé in my bedroom, a roommate who probably thought I was two weeks from eloping, and an entire empire of lies to maintain until Oskar Kristiansen kicked the bucket, whenever that might be. I couldn't let pesky *feelings* get in the way.

Finally, I stood, splashed cold water on my face, and forced myself to smile. When I failed to achieve what could pass as a genuine expression of nonchalance, I stopped trying.

Inhaling deeply, I decided we'd have to discuss everything tomorrow. Not now. Not when I felt so exposed, not when my desire felt this close to the surface, clamoring for attention and satisfaction and *him*.

Yes. *Tomorrow.* I nodded at my reflection in the mirror. *I'll figure it out tomorrow.*

* * *

Packing up my entire life took under three hours and only because I had a load of laundry to do. This fact made me either an ascetic or a minimalist. One sounded prudish, the other sounded chic, and neither prudish nor chic sounded like me.

By 9:30 AM, I'd consolidated all my possessions into four stackable plastic bins (with snap-tight lids), a single battered duffel, and my backpack. The task required so little time that by the end I found myself wandering the bare perimeter of my side of the room, mildly unnerved by its echo and emptiness. The blank walls and the empty desktop where my stuff had squatted for four years were bizarre to me. It was the first time in adulthood that I'd had the occasion to move out of a place and leave others behind. Usually, I was the one being left.

Was this a victory? Or a sign of my congenital inability to commit to physical objects and, by extension, people . . . ?

Whoa, whoa, whoa. That's too deep, Sam. Step away from the psychoanalysis paralysis and hop on over to the coping-strategy dance party.

I'd just dropped my last handful of hangers into the giveaway box when Nakita appeared at my door, arms laden with a plastic-wrapped bundle of bagels and a three-pack of full-sugar Red Bull. Her braids were looped into a crown on top of her head and she wore a tank top featuring a cat, also in a crown, captioned "Purr-fect."

"I got you some parting gifts, so—wow!" Nakita blinked into my room like she'd been expecting a mess. "That was fast. Did you burn all your stuff? Or do you only own, like, three shirts?"

I shrugged. "You know my secrets now. I rotate the same three outfits and use a cape for shock and awe. It's a trick I learned from Batman."

She deposited the bagels and drinks onto the edge of my now-empty desk. "You didn't even ask for help," she said, then spotted the empty closet and added, "I feel very weird about this."

"Don't feel weird. Feel wonderful." I waved a hand through the air dismissively. "Now you have one less person vying for the shower."

"Don't lie. You never showered."

"Hey!" I laughed, moving to hit her, and she stepped out of my reach before the back of my hand could connect.

She also laughed, but added, "This is all too sudden. And where did Andreas go? Is he coming back to help load and move stuff? I didn't see him leave."

Turning away from her and clearing my throat before speaking, I said, "He left super early, but he's arranged for movers. They'll be here around noon."

By the time I'd come back to the room last night, Andreas was already lying in my bed under the duvet, his back to the door. I'd thought about reminding him that I'd left a toothbrush out for his use, but decided against it. Minimizing interactions while in a dark room with two beds felt like the smarter option.

When I'd woken up after a fitful night's sleep, Andreas was gone, the clothes from Kendra's boyfriend were neatly folded on the bed, and the toothbrush in the bathroom was untouched, making me suspect he'd left in the middle of the night as soon as I'd fallen asleep. He had texted me this morning.

Andreas: Movers are arranged for today at noon. I will be home when you arrive, and we can scan your fingerprint for the door.

Presently, Nakita flopped backward onto my stripped mattress, arms out like she was about to make a snow angel. "So," she said, "how do you feel? Like, for real. I can't believe you're moving out, just like that." She snapped her fingers. "Have you told Diya?"

"I texted her. She hasn't messaged back." Diya hadn't responded to any of my texts since last night, which meant she was slammed.

The load of laundry I needed to do this morning consisted of Diya's sheets and my sheets. I'd slept in her bed. It only felt right to clean up my messes before I left.

"You texted her." Nakita voice was deadpan. She rolled her eyes at me. "You two have been roommates for four years and you texted her that you're leaving. Did she have any idea? About you and Andreas and how serious things were between you? Or will she be as shocked as I was when you told me this morning that you're moving out?"

"She'll be fine. I'm paying my share until a replacement can be found. If anything, she'll be thrilled to have a room to herself for a while." I tried not to let Nakita's words make me feel guilty.

It was true. Diya and I had been roommates for four years. That meant Diya knew how I was, how I didn't like getting attached. But it wasn't like I was leaving the country and would never see her again. I was moving fifteen blocks away—give or take a block.

Nakita's eyes moved over me. "How long have you two been dating, anyway? I thought for sure you'd never get married. And now you're engaged to a literal chess prodigy who is also, I cannot stress this enough, a billionaire's son. This is high-key the plot of a CW drama."

I snorted a laugh at her description. "Right? I keep expecting a team of lawyers to appear and offer me a check to walk away and never speak of it again." Though the statement was meant to sound like a joke, a team lawyers showing up to threaten me was definitely within the realm of possibility. In fact, I was sorta surprised one hadn't arrived yet.

Nakita grinned. "Or a film crew, or paparazzi. Just so you know, if a film crew offered me five hundred dollars, I would leak your entire internet search history. For science, obviously."

I sat next to her. "It doesn't feel real yet," I admitted, which was the truth. "It's like I'm watching someone else's life, but through my own eyes. Very out-of-body. Maybe it'll hit me when I see Andreas again."

"Hot take, but it's probably for the best," Nakita said, glancing sidelong at me. "If it were me, I'd already have blown up my social accounts, oversharing and bragging." Her face sobered. "You're good at being chill, Sam. Respect."

"I'm not chill," I said, looking at my own hands. "I'm just really, really good at pretending. My whole teenagerhood was, like, training for this moment.'"

Nakita's lips pressed into a line. "What do you mean? What was your adolescence like?"

I shrugged, staring forward. "When my dad died and we lost everything, the people who came after the bankruptcy judgment took everything. They even took the family photos on the wall—not for the pictures, but for the frames. My mother had to fight just to keep the photographs . . ." I blinked, realizing what I'd just said, how much I'd shared, and shifted my gaze to Nakita.

My words obviously surprised her. Nakita's mouth was open and her eyes were wide. I rarely told people about my family's financial apocalypse. Only Kaitlyn, and only after seven years of friendship.

Nakita sat up, cross-legged, and peered at me. "You never told me that."

"It's no big deal," I said dismissively and fiddled with the ring on my finger, twisting it around. My chest suddenly felt too tight and my stomach was sour. *Regret. This is oversharing regret.*

"It's ancient history." Standing once more, I lightened my tone. "I don't even think about it, but I guess . . . moral of the story: I don't get attached to things. If you only own stuff that fits in your suitcase, no one can take it from you."

Nakita's face did something that made my chest hurt even more. Standing also, she grabbed my hand and gave it a squeeze. "You know I was joking about selling your search history, right? Even if the paparazzi do come eventually, or reporters, I won't reveal anything."

I nodded, managing a close-lipped smile, but I didn't believe her. Nakita wasn't a bad person, and she was trustworthy to a point, but the allure of gossip was her Achillies' heel.

She increased the pressure of her fingers around mine. "And you know, you're allowed to keep things, right? You're allowed to have things, Sam."

Withdrawing my hand, I twisted to the side, making a show of stretching out my back. "I know. I'm just used to not wanting to keep things now, and it makes life so much tidier. Anyway! Let me finish cleaning in here, the movers should arrive soon." Walking around Nakita, I picked up my phone from the otherwise empty side table and checked the time.

Even with all my dillydallying while talking to Nakita, I still had over an hour until noon.

No word yet from Diya.

But that was fine. I would clean while the movers loaded my stuff, and would do my best to leave no traces of myself behind.

[15]

BINARY FISSION

Samantha

Nakita left when the movers arrived. They finished grabbing and loading everything in less than ten minutes. I knew they were used to working in the city because they'd double-parked, brazenly blocking the street rather than futilely hunting for a legitimate spot.

I finished cleaning around 12:15 PM. Checking my phone one last time for a message from Diya and finding none, I ultimately decided to head into work rather than go directly to Andreas's, telling myself I needed to get a jump start on cross-checking the citations for the upcoming conference presentation.

My decision to go to work had nothing at all to do with my desire to avoid seeing Andreas, but everything to do with my desire to avoid *talking* to Andreas.

The next time we spoke, I knew I'd have to put all my uncomfortable feelings out there, explain how I was attracted to him for reals, convince and assure him that mine was an unwilling and unwelcome attraction, and request we brainstorm how best to navigate this inconvenient situation moving forward.

For the record, I still hadn't given up hope that once we lived together, and I was exposed to all his unpleasant habits, thoughts, and beliefs, I might be cured of this unwieldy attraction.

If I was lucky, maybe he would cite the manosphere to justify a belief of why all mRNA vaccines were dangerous, or quote Grok as a reliable source of information about literally anything. If so, I would be cured of my attraction at once.

Or, even better, perhaps Andreas was an avid follower of Jordan Peterson or Andrew Tate. My repulsion would likely register on the Richter scale and I'd immediately go from giving him googly eyes to side-eyes. *Bing bang boom, shrivel my womb.*

Or, more effective, it would be great if he pontificated to me—a geneticist—that there exist only two genders, completely ignoring the existence of Turner's syndrome, androgen insensitivity syndrome, genetic steroid disorders, and science. And then it would be great if he called science or human rights a "political issue." That kind of thing would definitely do the trick. *Don't be cautious! Make me nauseous.*

Yeah. *Sigh.* Any and all of that would be so, so great. Convenient. And tidy.

To my surprise, as soon as I left my building, I spotted Tara waiting for me in her black Mercedes. I'd almost forgotten about her acting as my bodyguard and driver.

"If you're going to drive me everywhere from now on, I guess should join a gym." I met her eyes in the rearview mirror after settling in the back seat. She hadn't wanted me to sit in the front passenger seat, claiming the back seat was safer.

"Is walking to work the only exercise you get?" she asked, the corner of her mouth lifting.

"It is," I confirmed with a beleaguered sigh.

"Not a fan of gyms?"

"Not a fan of exercising just for the sake of exercising," I explained. "Makes me feel like a hamster. I played tennis in college, on scholarship. So, I don't mind training for a purpose, but not for, you know, health." I refrained from putting air quotes around the word *health,* but just barely.

I was the type of person who would spend all day cleaning a house without complaint, help an acquaintance move apartments, or walk a dog for hours, but couldn't find the motivation to get up from their desk for a breather, to take a mental break, or to stretch during the workday.

After a silence lasting two blocks, Tara said, "If you want, you could join my gym."

I stared at the back of her headrest and blurted stupidly, "You own a gym?"

Her eyes flickered back to me in the mirror, crinkling at the corners with a smile. "No. But I teach kickboxing at a gym. It's closer to Mr. Kristiansen's apartment than your previous address. Just let me know. You could try out a class. If you like it, join."

I stroked my chin like I had a wizard beard. "Kickboxing, eh? That sounds like a useful skill. When are you teaching next?"

"I'll text you a link to the schedule. Mr. Kristiansen sent me your number."

"Excellent," I murmured and tented my fingers, liking this notion more and more.

Andreas had warned me that his half brother Henrik preferred physical intimidation tactics over Tobias's mind-and-life-fuckery approach. Just the thought of learning how to effectively—should the opportunity present itself—kick Henrik in the face—or balls . . . _or both!_—brightened my mood.

Tara paused the Mercedes at the sidewalk next to my department building and, without cutting the engine, turned on her hazards. She then walked me to the entrance while sending me the promised link to her kickboxing class schedule. Before leaving me, Tara asked that I call or text ten minutes before I was ready to be picked up.

I saved her number in my phone and labeled her "Tara, Kickboxing Teacher." It felt less _Black Mirror_ or _Twilight Zone_ than "Tara, My Doppelganger Bodyguard."

Depositing my bag and clothes in my locker, I changed, badged into my work area, and quickly lost myself in converting all valid citations to ANSI/NISO standard terminology. I was so absorbed that when my phone buzzed, announcing a call, I sucked in a startled breath and almost choked on my saliva.

Diya's number flashed on my screen. I took a moment to gather my wits before answering, breathing out, then in, mostly to clear my airway. "Hello?"

"You're engaged? And you moved out? Have I entered an alternate timeline? Who was elected president?"

"Yes to the first two questions. I can't be certain regarding the last two questions."

I heard my roommate—er, former roommate—exhale a loud breath. "I know better than to ask too many questions. So, can you answer two more for me?"

"I'll do my best," I hedged and sat back in my office chair, feeling like I needed to mentally prepare myself.

"First, when can I see you? I'd like to say a proper goodbye. I like you, Sam, and I'll be honest"—she huffed a tired-sounding laugh—"I'm going to miss you—"

"Awww—"

"—and all the shirtless guys you used to parade around the apartment."

I snorted.

"CrossFit guy, we barely knew thee." The lingering smile in her voice was unmistakable. "Seriously, though. When can we get together? Let me buy you lunch or something."

My grin also persisted. "Absolutely. I'll send you some dates after the holiday." Spur of the moment, I suggested, "And we can try to make it a monthly thing. Sound good?" I wondered if I would later regret suggesting a standing lunch commitment, but I didn't think so.

I liked Diya, too. And I would miss her. She was good people.

"Sounds great," she said, the words almost obliterated by the sound of a siren from her side of the call.

I waited until the noise faded before asking, "What's the second question?"

"Are you happy?" She'd lowered her voice to ask this and I

detected a note of worry. "I mean, with Andreas. Does he make you happy? Do you actually want to marry him?"

For some reason, in that moment, I didn't want to lie to Diya. I didn't want to answer according to the plan just to get her off the phone. But I couldn't explain the complexities of my feelings either.

Thus, I settled on a version of the truth, both to ease her mind and to reduce my guilt. "Honestly, there is no one else in the world I could see myself marrying other than Andreas."

* * *

By the time I left the biology building, it was after 7:00 PM and my brain felt like a microwaved burrito: hot, overcooked, and liable to burst at the seams with one careless squeeze.

I called Tara from the women's locker room just before changing back into my normal clothes. Her black Mercedes idled at the curb when I exited the building, and I spotted her through the front wind-shield, brown hair pulled into a neat ponytail, the blue glow of her phone screen illuminating a face that looked enough like mine to make me do a double take.

She saw me and immediately killed the engine, opening the driver's-side door and stepping out into the cold. I waved, but before she could round the car, I opened the back door myself, tossed my backpack in, and then hesitated, half in and half out, caught by the friction of inertia. If I'd had a more poetic soul, I'd have called it "resistance to change." More accurately, it was the genetic legacy of a thousand generations of let's-just-wait-and-see-if-the-bear-leaves caution.

Eventually, I got in.

Tara adjusted the rearview and met my gaze. "Ready?" Her voice was unreasonably chipper. Probably all those kickboxing endorphins.

I wanted to say, *Define "ready."*

Instead, I said, "Sally forth."

She grinned, then pulled out into traffic. The silence between us was comfortable, like she understood that my primary need right now was mental preparation and recalibration.

I watched the city slide past, each streetlight blurring into the next. After three blocks of silence, I realized I'd been gripping my phone in my lap so tightly my hand had gone numb.

I turned the screen on: 7:14 PM. Zero new notifications. I was both relieved and irrationally disappointed that Andreas hadn't texted me since this morning.

Perhaps he hadn't texted because he knew where I was. Tara, as my shadow, had likely filled him in. I considered this, that Tara and any other bodyguard assigned to me would probably be reporting my movements to Andreas.

This thought didn't make me resent Tara. It didn't even make me resent Andreas. It made me resent Oskar, Tobias, and Henrik for being societal sepsis. If only Oskar hadn't been an evil, greedy little virus of a humanoid, perhaps—

Perhaps Andreas and I would be getting engaged for real . . . ?

I rolled my eyes at myself and shook my head. Alternate universe, indeed.

After I'd finished working on the citations, I'd spent an hour helping Dmitry troubleshoot a genetics pipeline issue he'd emailed me about last week but I'd been too deep in my own drama to reply. There was also a backlog of Hauser's undergrad lab reports to grade, which was not technically my job anymore but felt like an anchor to the world I was rapidly losing.

Time collapsed. At some point I ran samples in the secure lab and cleaned up after myself with military precision, mostly because I knew the next person to use the space would be me again, and if I left a mess, it would just be my own future self who suffered. I liked to think of it as a recursive act of kindness.

All day, I'd been stalling. And now, in the darkness of Tara's back seat, I was still stalling. Waiting for me at the end of this ride was an uncomfortable conversation about feelings—*great, yay feelings*—and a new, likely jarring, shift in my reality. I'd never met anyone who embraced sudden shifts in reality without some instinctive resistance and at least a little crankiness.

Tara pulled up to the curb outside Andreas's building. She didn't immediately reach for the locks or say goodbye. Instead, she turned around, elbow draped over the back of her seat, and looked at me with a subtle intensity.

"You okay?" she asked.

"Sure," I said, then, after a beat, "I've been worse."

She laughed, low and genuine. "Want me to walk you up?"

"No," I said, then caught myself. "Yes. Wait—no, I'm fine. I've been here before."

She nodded, studying me. "Okay," she said, but didn't move to start the car again. "Text me if you need anything. I'll be in the garage across the street until ten."

I gave her a thumbs-up, but my hand trembled so badly I had to turn it into a wave. I fumbled the handle, stepped out, and closed the door with a gentleness that sounded like an apology.

At the entrance, the doorman clocked me immediately. He gave a curt nod, then opened the door before I could even raise a hand in greeting.

"Good evening, Ms. Jarlston," he said. The way he pronounced my name was clinical, almost like it was a password. "Welcome home."

I wanted to correct him—explain that I wasn't really "home," I was just "here," and only because of a paperwork anomaly and a series of questionable life choices. Instead, I nodded, mumbled a thank-you, and walked through the vestibule.

The last time I'd been here, Andreas held my hand, and I remembered the exact pressure of his palm and the scent of his coat, and how it made me feel weirdly exposed and helpless. I shook the memory loose and marched to the elevator, punched in the code Andreas had given me, and rode in silence to the penthouse. I made a game of staring at my own reflection in the mirrored walls, trying to will my face into something more serenely composed and less emotionally constipated.

When I stepped out, the hallway was empty. I hovered outside the apartment door for a full minute, rehearsing different greetings in my head, then finally raised my hand to ring the bell.

The door opened before I could touch it.

Standing in the doorway was a tall, broad-shouldered guy with pale blond hair and blue eyes so bright they were legit alarming. He wore mesh basketball shorts and a slightly sweat-dampened long-sleeved T-shirt, and looked like he'd stepped straight out of *Prep-School Quarterly* (not a real newspaper as far as I knew; but if it existed, this guy would be their spokesperson, founder, and president).

I blinked, taking an involuntary step backward. "Uh, hi?"

The man smiled, a tiny curve of his lips. "You must be Samantha?" His accent was subtle, American Southern.

"That's me," I said. "Who's asking?"

He stepped aside, and gestured for me to come in. "Roman. A friend of Andreas's."

From somewhere deep in the apartment, a female voice with a faint British-sounding accent called out, "He's not a friend. They're archrivals."

My eyebrows nearly shot off my forehead. Roman gave me a small, conspiratorial smile, then leaned in to stage-whisper, "We're not actually rivals. But the internet thinks we are."

A woman appeared at the end of the entryway, drying her hands on a towel. She was petite and sharp-boned, with thick, long black hair pulled into a high ponytail and a beauty mark perfectly placed below her right eye. She wore black yoga pants and a gray exercise shirt. Even in casual wear, she radiated a kind of intimidating composure that made me instantly want to look up and listen to her TED Talk. Assuming she had a TED Talk.

"Hi." She offered her pale hand. "I'm Jackie Cheng."

I shook it. Her grip was precise, not too firm, not too soft.

"Nice to meet you," I said a bit robotically, only because I'd already been overwhelmed prior to entering the apartment. And now, suddenly faced with unexpected *people*, my nerves were fraying.

Jackie held on to my hand a beat longer than necessary, then pulled me into the apartment with a smooth, practiced motion. "Come in,

Andreas is in the shower. We just got back from the gym. Roman insisted we had to squeeze in one last session before his curfew."

"Curfew?" I repeated, not sure if I was missing a joke.

Roman nodded. "I have to check in with my host family at ten sharp, or they send out the search party." He said it with a straight face, so it was either true or a level of deadpan I could only aspire to.

Jackie rolled her eyes. "He's in town for a few days, doing a chess camp with the local kids. They treat him like he's a big celebrity or something."

"I'm not a celebrity," Roman grumbled.

Jackie ignored him and steered me into the living area. "Sit down. Want some water? Juice? I think there's kombucha, but it's homemade."

I perched on the edge of the couch. "Water's good, thanks." After I said the words, I marveled at the fact that this woman had just offered me something to drink in the apartment where I was now currently living. *Ahhhh! New realities suck!*

Roman sat at the far end of the sofa, angled toward me but not so close as to invade my space. He watched me with a kind of directness I found both flattering and disorienting.

Jackie disappeared into the kitchen, then called back, "How was your day, Samantha?"

I thought about the hours spent hiding in the biology building, the way my stomach had twisted all day in anticipation of this very moment, only to find Andreas's friends welcoming me instead of my fake fiancé.

"Uneventful," I said. "How about you? Did you, uh, have a nice day?"

Look at me, chitchatting like a chitchatter. Would wonders never cease?

Jackie returned with three glasses of water, handed one to me, one to Roman, and kept the third. "You work in genetics, right? PhD candidate?"

"Yes," I said, surprised she knew so much about me. "Final year. Or it should be."

Roman sipped his water, then asked, "What is your dissertation about?"

I blinked at the question, thrown by how sincerely interested he sounded. "Uhh. Well, originally, it was epigenetic markers of stress inheritance in CRISPR-edited lines of drosophila."

Jackie made a face of pure delight. "Ooh, I love fruit fly people. They're always the most dramatic at conferences. Nothing like a five-millimeter bug to turn a scientist into a gladiator."

I found myself laughing even though her words confused me. "I'm not sure what that means. But, um, I changed my focus after one year. My dissertation is now on bioremediation of ocean plastics via genetically modified microbes."

"Oh. Cool. Isn't the island of trash in the Pacific Ocean larger than Texas? Or is that a made-up fact? Where did I read that?" Jackie pointed her gaze at Roman. "He's the real scientist here. Chess is just his side-hustle."

Roman's mouth tugged up on one side. "I'm not a scientist. But I do like puzzles."

Jackie rolled her eyes, like his statement was a shared joke. I decided I liked Jackie a lot, and Roman maybe even more, but in a way that was less "be friends" and more "he's interesting to observe."

"So"—Jackie sunk into the armchair across from me—"do couples in America typically move in together only after getting engaged?"

My mouth went dry, her question catching me off guard. For some reason, I felt wholly unprepared to discuss the American societal norms surrounding engagements.

Roman bailed me out. "There's no such thing as typical in the USA. Some folks wait until marriage to move in together, some wait 'til engagement. Some move in without ever planning to get married at all."

Jackie nodded, absorbing this information, then glanced at me. Perhaps she misread my wide eyes as confusion because she explained, "I'm from Singapore. We sometimes have marriage requirements surrounding housing. Or rather, before applying for a flat. Sorry. I was just curious."

Roman grinned, a tiny flash of teeth. "Jackie travels a lot, but doesn't get out much."

She wrinkled her nose at him. "This is my first time to the USA and I don't want to take for granted that American television is indicative of reality."

"It's not," both Roman and I said in unison, then the three of us shared a grin, with Roman adding, "Especially—ironically—reality television. Reality television is less reflective of American society than most scripted TV."

"What a relief," Jackie chuckled.

Feeling myself relax a bit, I took another sip of water and floundered for an acceptable subject to discuss with Andreas's friends even as curiosity swelled within me. I surmised that Roman and Andreas competed against each other in tournaments and were colleagues. But how did Jackie fit in?

Before I could figure out how to frame the question casually rather than blurt out, *How do you know Andreas? Are you good friends? How long have you known each other? Did you date?* Jackie glanced at her watch, then abruptly stood up.

"Shoot, we have to run. Roman's curfew is real. And I have an online match at eleven."

Roman also stood and turned to me with a small smile. "It was nice meeting you, Samantha."

"You, too." I set my water glass on a coaster and straightened from the couch, wondering if I should walk them out.

I should, right? Technically, I live here. It would be polite.

While I was still engaging in my internal debate, Jackie crossed to me and pulled me in for a brief hug, saying as she leaned away, "Andreas said if he was still in the shower when you got here, to give you this." She handed me a sealed envelope that she'd seemingly pulled out of thin air. "Instructions, probably. He loves instructions."

I took it, a little surprised at the weight of it. "Oh . . . thanks," I said, but she and Roman had already left the room, walking themselves out.

I waited until I heard the door snick shut before I opened the envelope.

Inside was a printout, double-sided, with a list of building employees, hours for amenities, the procedure for picking up packages, and emergency phone numbers for the night managers and staff. At the bottom, in Andreas's neat, all-caps handwriting, it read:

We need to program your thumbprint into the door pad tonight so you can come and go as you please. I had your things placed in the main bedroom, which is off the living room to the south. —A

He gave me the main bedroom? I frowned at the note, reading it again. The fact that he'd given me the main bedroom—which had likely been his bedroom—was at once confusing and irritating. Was he trying to be chivalrous? Now I'd have to live and sleep in a room that likely smelled like him.

I exhaled. The silence in the apartment felt heavy.

I thought about refusing the main bedroom, potentially sleeping on the couch tonight, but that seemed juvenile. Instead, I walked to the room he wanted me to take and peeked inside.

The movers had delivered my things. They were stacked neatly against the wall, untouched. The bed—a California king—was covered in an off-white-and-pink duvet cover that didn't belong to me. It looked expensive, maybe mulberry silk? The furniture also looked expensive, a minimalist yet sturdy maple. The walls were the color of sandstone and appeared to be paneled with fabric. Or perhaps an extremely high-end wallpaper. The light and airy aura of this room struck me as extremely different from the apartment's entry and living rooms, with their dark red antique carpets, floor-to-ceiling paintings, dramatic leather couches, and dark wood furniture.

In contrast, this space felt undecorated, a blank canvas with tasteful, subtle bones. It didn't feel empty or cold. Rather, it felt warm and ready. *Huh.*

Meandering further inside, I noted that this bedroom was likely bigger than the entirety of my previous apartment, the one I'd shared with three roommates. A view of the city through floor-to-ceiling windows contributed to the sense of expansiveness. My attention fell on white closet doors, currently closed and gleaming with the promise of a storage space I would never fill.

Frowning thoughtfully, I sat on the bed, unsurprised to find the duvet was fluffy and feather, and the mattress was heavenly. Conflicted, I let my mind go blank.

This is my life now. This is where I live. Even if I didn't accept the main bedroom, I would be living here, in this ridiculously huge apartment with my ridiculously attractive fake fiancé, for an undetermined period of time.

I was about to check my phone for the time—somehow, I was convinced it was way later than it actually was—when I heard a door open from somewhere in the apartment followed by approaching footsteps.

I stood, braced myself, and walked back into the living room.

Abruptly halting mid-step, I grimaced at the offensively gorgeous sight before me. Andreas appeared from the opposite hallway, hair damp, a black T-shirt clinging to the muscles of his shoulders, and— you guessed it—a pair of soft gray sweatpants low on his hips.

Well, well, well. *Lucky me.*

Swallowing a mouthful of lusty saliva, I fought a laugh as I cast my eyes heavenward. Was he trying to seduce me? Probably not. Was I seduced? Undoubtedly so.

"When did you arrive?" he asked, voice even but pitched low.

I swallowed, feeling my own pulse thud in my throat, and forced myself to meet his beautiful green eyes. "Just now. Jackie and Roman let me in. And Jackie gave me the envelope."

He nodded, then leaned against the large, black circular table set by the window, still applying a towel to his hair. "Did you have dinner?"

I opened my mouth to respond but then snapped it shut, needing to think for a moment. *Wait. Did I have dinner?*

"Does a bag of Goldfish count?"

He made a face. "Are you hungry?"

Instinct wanted to turn his question into a double entendre and approximately one hundred suggestive retorts floated through my brain. Some were cheesy, a la, *For you? Yes.* And some were sensually ambiguous, such as, *Only if it tastes good.*

I stymied the reflex, saying instead, "Caloric sustenance would not be rejected," which might've been the least sexy reply in the universe. And that was the point.

Lifting an eyebrow at my response, Andreas seemed to fight a smile. "I ordered food. It should be here soon. If you are hungry, there will be more than enough to share."

Was I hungry? I couldn't tell. All I felt was the weird, humming tension that had followed me all day, and the urge to say something— anything—that would make the next moment easier.

But there was no easy. There was only the truth.

Gathering a deep breath, I squared my shoulders and said, "We should talk."

Andreas didn't move, but his eyes sharpened. "Now?"

"Yes," I said, because if I didn't do it now, I never would.

"Okay. Let's talk," he said, blinking once, slowly, giving me the impression he'd expected this.

Or perhaps, he'd been anticipating it.

[16]
CELL REPRODUCTION: MITOSIS

Samantha

I felt . . . uncomfortable.

Presently, we sat at the same black, circular table where I'd reviewed the adoption paperwork and where we'd discussed the initial stages of our plan, the details of the smoke screen, and our conditions for the subterfuge. Thinking back, I marveled at my previous bold aplomb, showing up here in a skintight dress and stilettos, demanding that we get down to business.

Tonight, the dynamic felt incredibly different, and yet also exactly the same, which made no sense.

Peeking at Andreas, I took note of how his gaze moved over me now, dressed as I was in an old baggy T-shirt and equally baggy ripped jeans. His eyes held the same flavor of intensity as before. And this realization gave my usually imperturbable heart spikes of pause, confusion, and panic.

And that's when the doubt crept in. *Perhaps I assumed too much that night.*

Glancing down at my T-shirt, I confirmed it was not at all sexy. I frowned and peered at him again, a new hypothesis forming, leading to a new conclusion. *Perhaps this is not heat and interest in his gaze at all, but rather this is simply his normal expression . . . ?*

Had I misinterpreted his interest two nights ago, and then again during our fake engagement dinner? Was this attraction I felt entirely one-sided? I swallowed around a parched throat, my previously controlled thoughts bouncing around the inside of my head like Ping-Pong balls.

"You wanted to talk." Andreas's flat statement pulled me out of my queasy contemplations.

I nodded. "Yes. Yes, that's right." Folding my hands on the table-top, I couldn't help but continue to study him.

His gaze felt laser focused on me, and just as hot as it had two nights ago. And yet, after the long day I'd had, I knew I looked like an untidy, dusty, tired mess.

What is going on?

Andreas dipped his chin and raised his eyebrows. "Samantha? Are you well?"

I nodded again, bringing my hands to my lap where I could twist my fingers without him seeing.

Forget it. Who cares if the attraction is one-sided. All you need to do is tell him that you find him irresistibly attractive, you have real feelings for him, and ask him to help you get rid of these feelings.

Inhaling deeply for courage, I mentally prepared myself for the necessary words, but instead what I said was, "So, Andreas. What are your thoughts on Jordan Peterson?"

Andreas's expression changed from what I'd previously—and potentially, incorrectly—labeled as *hot and interested* to *bemused* with a single blink. "Pardon? Who is that?"

I twisted my mouth to the side. "You don't know who Jordan Peterson is?"

"No." His gaze flickered over me. "Should I?"

"What about Andrew Tate? Ring any bells?"

"No." There was no recognition in his eyes. "Are you considering them for roles at Genetix? Are they scientists?"

Frowning dejectedly, I shook my head. "Not even a little."

"Then, who are—"

"Forget it." I waved a hand in the air, batting away any follow-up questions, then let it drop. "Tell me, what are your thoughts on mRNA vaccines?"

He blinked twice, once more looking bemused. "Uh, I do not—I mean, should I not be asking you?"

"What is that supposed to mean?" I searched his words for a possible offensive meaning and frustratingly found none.

"You are the geneticist and know more about this subject than me." When I continued to glare at him, he added, "What I mean is, I play chess for a living, an occupation that has nothing to do with medical science. Why would I think I know more about mRNA vaccines than a PhD candidate in genetics? That would make me a fool."

I nibbled the inside of my bottom lip, growing more and more irritated by his lack of delusions of grandeur and his trust in highly educated experts. "Fine," I bit out. "Then, how about, where do you stand politically on racism, as an example."

He frowned at me, visibly confused, and exhaled a short laugh. "Okay, racism is not a political issue. It is a moral, ethical, human-rights, fear-based, lack-of-education issue, and should not be justified or condoned by political affiliation."

Huffing, I gritted my teeth and turned my head away from his stupid handsome face. He had to possess at least one reprehensible, and therefore unattractive, opinion. Why couldn't he just *cooperate?!?!!*

"Who is your . . . favorite . . . member of The Beatles?"

Now he narrowed his eyes on me, the side of his mouth tugging slightly upward. "George Harrison."

DAMN IT!

"What about BTS?"

"RM or V."

My lungs filled with the fire of exasperation because no one was this perfect. Placing my hands flat on the table, I leaned forward, preparing a rapid-fire question assault.

"Favorite flavor of ice cream."

"Chocolate."

I made a face, surprised. "Really?"

"Yes, vegan cashew chocolate ice cream is the best of the vegan flavors."

I didn't have any experience with vegan ice cream, so I moved on. "Charles Darwin or Karl Marx?"

"Darwin," he answered immediately. "In my opinion, Marx misinterpreted natural selection to justify his philosophical and political ideologies."

"Dog or cat?"

"Both. If you recall, I love animals."

Shoot. That's right. Unable to stop the question, I asked, "Is that why you're vegan? Because you love animals?"

"No. Not really. It is mainly for health reasons." He seemed to hesitate before continuing. "My mother died of colon cancer when I was eleven, she was just thirty-two. And her father died of colon cancer at twenty-nine."

"Oh, Andreas." My hand came to my chest where a sudden ache had made breathing difficult. "I'm so sorry. I didn't know about your mom." I fought the urge to rush over and hug him.

He shook his head, jaw clenching, and dismissed my concern. "It was a long time ago. But peer-reviewed studies have shown that a vegan diet greatly reduces the risk of colon cancer. Also, honestly, I do not enjoy the taste of meat or dairy."

GAH! He'd mentioned *peer-reviewed* studies, not just *research studies.* Get a load of the size of this guy's media literacy, ladies. *Be still my heart.*

But he'd also mentioned not liking dairy, and that was something I could work with. "Not even cheese?" I questioned. "You're telling me you don't like a good Camembert? Nothing alluring about Gouda? Really?"

He gave me a small smile. "No."

I examined Andreas for a long moment, wondering if his opinion about cheese was enough to temper my attraction to him. *Unfortunately, it's not enough.* Andreas was more beautiful, smarter, and cooler than my affinity for cheese, shockingly.

Now, if only he would say something rude about coffee . . . But no. The first time we met weeks ago he'd ordered coffee. He liked coffee.

Sitting back in my chair, I rubbed my forehead. This was getting me nowhere.

Desperate, I tried for a more direct approach. "Tell me something, Andreas."

"What would you like to know?"

"Tell me something unlikable about yourself." I peeked at him, letting my hand drop to my lap again.

His eyes were on me, but they were unfocused, like he was in deep contemplation, attempting to decipher the riddle of my question.

"I do not und—"

"I'll start." I crossed my arms and leveled him with a frank look. "I still like watching old movies even though—when viewed through today's lens—they are often incredibly problematic. I don't care. I still like watching them. In fact, I enjoy the heck out of *Some Like It Hot* and I do not care that some people tell me it's high-key sexist and homophobic. See? I'm a terrible person."

Andreas's eyebrows lifted until his forehead wrinkled. "I do not think that makes you a terrible per—"

"Also, when I'm really busy, I don't shower for days and days." I gave him a flat look. "Sometimes longer than a week, and I kinda like the smell of my own stink."

His eyes widened and he snapped his mouth shut.

"Gross, right?" I wasn't finished. "I would rather be late for a party than arrive on time, but without makeup. I hate going to parties without wearing makeup, but I procrastinate putting it on, which means I'm often late. Yet, I'll likely never change this about myself. Also, I forget to check my mail and have a bad habit of missing important documents and letters, letting them pile up for over a month. I don't enjoy small talk and usually refuse to do it. This means I frequently come across as abrupt or judgy, and I'm really okay with that." I paused, thought about that last one, then added, "Probably because I am both abrupt and judgy, so that's on me. But, again, I'm okay with that."

Andreas had leaned forward as I spoke and placed an elbow on the table. Most of his mouth and chin were obscured by his hand, his thumb and forefinger resting to either side of his nose. His half-lidded gaze seemed to bore into me, giving me the impression that he was listening intently.

"Let's see, what else . . ." I tapped my chin. "Uh, sometimes people don't like my face, or my aura, or my vibes. I get that a lot. I know I sometimes say really stupid and ignorant things. But since that's something everyone does, I'll give myself a pass and try to do better. I also get mad and vindictive when I feel slighted or taken advantage of. Oh! I drink too much coffee and then complain when I have trouble sleeping at night. I also doomscroll on my phone if I have insomnia, and then complain even more about having trouble sleeping at night. It's insufferable."

"You have trouble sleeping at night?" Andreas tilted his head slightly to the side.

"Yes. But here's another one. I suffer from making the fundamental attribution error *all the time*. You know, that thing people do where their own mistakes can be explained away by circumstances outside of their control, but then they unilaterally decide other people's mistakes are obviously due to faulty character traits? I do that. I actually really hate this about myself and I've gotten so much better about recognizing it as I've aged." I looked up at the ceiling, thinking the matter over. "So, let's call that a half-unlikable thing."

Andreas made a short sound, pulling my attention back to him.

His hand fell away from his mouth. "Samantha, why are you telling me all this?"

"Because I want you to tell me something unlikable about yourself, so I figured I would share first."

"Why? Why do you want to know something unlikable about me?"

I stared at Andreas, hoping he'd simply play along without making me explain myself. I stared for so long, I was forced to blink several times. And still he returned my stare, seemingly content to wait me out.

Well, this flex of superhuman patience is certainly unlikable.

Eventually, I glanced away, my eyes moving over the interior of his apartment while my attention shifted inward. No more stalling. I was going to have to tell him about my unwelcome feelings, about this attraction I didn't want and for which I needed his help dispelling. There was no getting around saying it now.

"So, here's the thing." I crossed my arms again, determined to approach this subject as analytically and dispassionately as possible. I could not, however, immediately lift my eyes higher than the tabletop. "As it turns out, and quite against my will, I find myself in a precarious situation."

Hazarding a glance, I noted how his gaze had grown narrowed and powerfully intent. I didn't miss how Andreas leaned forward. Nor did I miss how wooden and useless my tongue felt, and how dry my mouth was, and how courage was beginning to taste like cowardice.

And yet, despite the sudden sweatiness of my palms, I forced myself to continue, because I was an adult. "And I fully admit, I am to blame, obviously. Feelings aren't facts, but they exist, nevertheless"—I swallowed convulsively, telling myself to slow down even as words cascaded out of me like a waterfall—"and despite my attempts to neutralize this—this issue, sometimes emotions exist outside of the Venn diagram of intentions and willful choices. And so, what I want to make you aware of before things take an unintentional turn for—"

The sound of the front door chime cut off my rapid monologue and I flinched, my eyes darting toward the entryway. Despite my best efforts, my heart had taken off at a gallop and I suddenly became aware that my stomach was swimming. *Ugh. I feel like I'm going to throw up.*

"The food." Andreas sounded mildly irritated by the interruption. He pushed away from the table and straightened slowly. "I will be right back. Do not leave."

I nodded automatically. But then, as soon as he disappeared from view, I asked myself via a whisper spoken out loud, "What the hell am I doing?"

Was I really going to confess like this? I'd never confessed having feelings to anyone because I'd never caught feelings before that were worth confessing. Who the hell did I think I was?

Placing my palm over my now thundering heart and staring

forward, my brain began to bargain and advocate for an alternate course of action. Because this was freaking *scary*.

It felt like . . .

It feels like . . .

Like what I imagined a wild animal felt when their paw was stuck in the jaws of a steel trap. Was I really going to wait for the hunter to return and explain with reason and logic how I didn't want my paw to be stuck in a steel trap, and would he please release me so that I could go back to being free and wild?

NO!

No, absolutely not. An animal does not try to reason with a hunter. Worst-case scenario, the hunter felt sorry for the animal and shot it on sight. Whereas, best-case scenario . . .

Wait.

Who was I kidding? There was no best case! Was I insane?

I stood abruptly from the table, the chair making a muffled sound on the red carpet as it fell over behind me. Andreas reentered the room, two tied plastic bags dangling from his fingertips, and froze mid-stride when he spotted me and the toppled chair.

A pause, then, "Are you okay?"

I nodded, sucking in oxygen as I turned and forced my fingers and arms to right the chair. "Mm-hmm. I'm fine. I'm good."

Haltingly, he asked, "Do you want to eat now? Or we can wait."

I closed one eye, scrunching my face. "Um, you know—" I stopped myself and cleared my throat because the two words had arrived extremely high-pitched. Remodulating my voice, I tried again. "I'm not hungry. But you should eat."

My mind thrashed around in my own stupidity, struggling to find a viable point to make, one that could take the place of my scary confession.

"Are you sure?" Andreas closed the distance to the table and set the bags on its surface. "I ordered quite a lot."

"I'm sure." I nodded tightly, my brain finally latching on to an alternate argument in place of my inadvisable admission of *feelings*. "I can talk while you eat."

His eyes moved over me, his expression quizzical. But all he said was, "Okay," as he reclaimed his seat.

I did not sit. I had too much adrenaline coursing through my system.

Instead, I folded my arms over my chest like armor and lifted my chin. "All I was saying was that I don't think it's right for me to take the main bedroom. This is your apartment and that room is too big for me and I don't think it makes any sense for me to take the main bedroom when this is your apartment, after all. I'd like to move my stuff into one of the other rooms and sleep there. Tonight. If that's okay. That'll save us from having to change sheets in the morning."

Andreas had begun untying the knot in one of the bags as he sat. But by the time I'd finished speaking, his hands were still and his eyes were affixed forward. Silence engulfed us, making me feel like I'd been swallowed by a sea creature that excreted awkwardness as a pheromone.

I watched his chest rise and fall, listening to the slightly stunted yet audible sound of his exhale. He seemed to be parsing through my words again, evaluating them, maybe searching for hidden meanings. Who knows?

I'd tricked myself two nights ago, believing I knew what he'd been thinking, and now I was paying the price with pride as my currency. Like hell would I assume I knew what he was thinking ever again.

At length, Andreas abandoned the bag and stood, slowly lifting his eyes to mine. "This is what you wanted to talk about?" His voice was oddly gruff.

I nodded.

His jaw seemed to work, giving me the impression he was running the tip of his tongue over his back teeth. His chest rose and fell again, another audible sigh. "Pick any room you like," he said, the words low and rumbly.

"Oh. Thank you." I kept on nodding. "I will."

Refocusing his attention on the food, he frowned. But instead of untying the knot, he picked up the two bags and strolled away toward the kitchen. As soon as he disappeared from view, I slouched, allowing myself a quick moment of relief and reprieve.

A breathy laugh tumbled out of me. *Yikes*. That had been close. Thank goodness I'd stopped myself.

Fascinatingly, the sudden sensation of relief was enough to buoy my spirits anew, because I was nothing if not a problem solver. I didn't need Andreas to help me fix my attraction. I could do it myself. I'd relied on no one but myself for a long, long, *long* time. I loved Kaitlyn, but I didn't actually need her.

Yeah. That's right. I'll do it myself.

I would figure this out and mercilessly cauterize it before I allowed anything as frivolous as attraction to interfere. I didn't need Andreas to expose his unlikable traits, fixing myself wasn't his responsibility. I simply needed to focus on what really mattered.

Revenge.

For my dad, for my mom, for myself. Everything else should be background noise.

Determined, I strolled to the main bedroom with my head high and grabbed my suitcase. It contained all my clothes and toiletries, everything I needed for tonight and tomorrow. The rest I could grab at some point later, or leave in the bins. No use unpacking more than necessary, no reason to settle in.

I would pick a different room and leave Andreas to his palatial suite. It didn't matter where I slept as long as I didn't let myself get too comfortable.

This, him, his apartment, it was all temporary.

Yes, best for both of us if I reminded myself of this fact rather than burden Andreas with my irrelevant feelings.

[17]

FROM FOSSILS TO NEO-DARWINISM

Andreas

Sleep would not come. Not for lack of exhaustion. Nor for lack of opportunity.

The real, unpalatable explanation: Samantha slept here, under my roof, and now every nerve within my body had chosen to organize itself around her proximity, like a citywide blackout except for the single column of light that burned for her, and only her. There existed not enough darkness in the world to convince my body to power down.

Two hours since she'd retired to her room, two hours since I'd heard her methodically moving her shampoo and other items into the hall bathroom, and yet the sum of my progress toward sleep was nil. I lay on my back, eyes fixed on the stippled darkness of the ceiling, and forced myself to replay old chess matches, then count backward from one hundred, then a thousand, then attempt the old trick of imagining myself on a frozen lake, letting the silent cold and emptiness smooth my thoughts into nothing.

Didn't work. In the end, I tried imagining myself as the ice, and she was the body of water below, forever churning, breaking, threatening to warm, melt, and consume me.

Unsurprisingly, this did nothing to propel me toward sleep.

Every five minutes, I checked my phone, hoping for a trivial update from any of the night staff, or, failing that, some sign of familial unrest that might require my attention and thus distract me from the problem at hand. My notifications remained empty.

Earlier, when I wasn't cataloguing the sounds of Sam's movements —shower, teeth, changing, light on, light off—I reviewed the order of the previous night's events as we'd faked our engagement, frame by frame, rewinding over every minute detail. The way she looked at me across the table, the tremor in her hands, her voice when she told me to expect tongue, the impossible heat of her body in my lap at her apartment. Her eyes and smile when she laughed.

She'd always laughed easily. As a child, she'd howled at every low-effort joke, even the ones meant to sting, tossed at her by my brothers. But that laughter had been a type of rebellion.

Making her laugh—truly laugh—used to be the most reliable method of pulling her out of a dark mood. I'd spent hours, sometimes days, strategizing and arranging situations to make her laugh. And when she did, when my well-laid plans came to fruition, it had always made me feel . . . powerful. In a way that wasn't about control, but about being seen. And appreciated. And enjoyed. Useful. Now, I missed it.

I missed her.

Last night, I'd caught only glimpses of it—her laugh, her joy— through a wineglass filled with rosé, darkly, and only when she felt safe enough to lower her guard. The rest of our time together, she'd been tense, wary. I remained convinced she still distrusted me. Or, at the very least, she did not wish to be alone with me.

If she'd asked, I would've left the city, the country, the planet, just to prove she could feel safe here.

She'd chosen the farthest bedroom from mine. The "service suite," a twenty-square-meter room designed for a housekeeper or a guest I'd never invited. She'd taken her suitcase across the threshold and closed the door with a finality that felt less like a boundary and more like a verdict.

I wasn't a fool. My opening strategy had been clumsy, assumed too much after too many years apart. But this second strategy, adopting her as my plan B, had backfired. I shouldn't have cared about the distance between our bedroom doors, but I did.

I wanted her to want this room. It had been stripped and redecorated. I'd arranged for a designer while I attended meetings, interviews, and practice sessions yesterday and today. I'd instructed them to discard anything Samantha might notice or object to, to make the space a blank slate for her. I wanted her to feel comfortable changing anything and everything to her liking, paint the walls, break the windows, gut the closet. I wanted her to possess whatever wanted, including a sense of control.

Including me, in the unlikely event. . .

Abruptly, I realized I was hard, embarrassingly so, and rolled to my side to hide it from no one. I told myself I should go for a run downstairs in the gym, burn off the excess energy, or take a cold shower. I didn't move. I couldn't. Thoughts of her in that black dress from two nights ago had me reaching under the covers and inside my pants.

A door shut softly, somewhere down the hall. I stilled and listened. A beat passed. The silence like a held breath.

Waiting, rigid and alert, all my attention funneled down the hallway, anticipating her next move. Nothing happened. A full fifteen minutes passed, maybe more. Time became elastic, every second stretching into an eternity.

It must've been after two when I heard the creak of a floorboard beyond my door. Not loud enough for the average person to notice, but I'd spent enough hours in this apartment to form a familiarity with every minor defect. My heart doubled its pace, then tripled. I endeavored to control my breathing, to calm the surging blood in my veins.

The knob on my door turned, ever so slowly. The door opened enough to allow a slip of dim light from the living room, which added to the city lights coming in from the large window. For a second, nothing. Then she was there.

Samantha stood in the doorway, silhouetted in her oversized shirt, hair down around her face and shoulders, eyes half open. Her feet bare and her posture strange, a little slack, as though this room's gravity were heavier than the rest of the world's. She did not speak.

I sat up in bed, all the air gone from my lungs, and managed, "Samantha?"

She did not respond, instead shuffling into the room, not quite looking at me, gaze pointed just above my head. Samantha paused at the end of the bed, hands loose at her sides, then climbed up—one knee on the mattress, then the other—and crawled over the covers until she drew even with me.

Stunned, my body did not know what to do. My brain had already been spun into glass, and now I suspected that, at any movement, the entire scene might shatter into a dream.

Samantha lay beside me, facing me, close enough that I could see the sheen of sweat on her temple. She burrowed into the pillow. Then, with a kind of delicate desperation, curled herself against my body. Her leg wormed between mine, and her hand found its way to my stomach beneath my shirt. Her breath was warm on my throat.

All the muscles in my body tensed at once, locked in a state of absolute incredulity.

She pressed her face against the side of my neck and let out a long, shaky exhale, then, as if it were the most natural thing in the world, she relaxed completely, melting into me.

I did not breathe. I did not move.

This was the opposite of anything I'd ever imagined. In every scenario where she ended up in my bed, it had been a complete fantasy, divorced from reality. What else could it have been? Sleepwalking? Which—wait.

Hold on.

Is Samantha sleepwalking?

A wave of suspicion broke over the shock and arousal. Her roommate had mentioned that Samantha sleepwalked. Certainly, she wasn't awake now. Had she come here on purpose, to tell me something, to ask for something?

If I said her name again, would she hear me?

I swallowed, felt her arm tense at the subtle movement, and risked it. "Samantha?"

No verbal response.

Instead, she tightened her grip around my chest, and slid her hand further under the hem of my shirt such that her palm pressed flat to my stomach, hot and real. I wanted to capture her hand and move it lower. I wanted to entangle our fingers together and slide them into her underwear.

I wanted to roll on top of her, strip her naked, kneel between her thighs, and devour her whole.

But I did nothing. I remained still.

She wore a shirt—baggy, covered in cartoon blobs that were likely science based. I focused on the pattern as a mental distraction. Her thigh, bare and warm, pressed tight to my leg. The pressure of her head on my shoulder, the weight of her body draped over me, felt somehow urgent.

Samantha's breathing evened out. After a minute, I recognized the pattern. Deep inhale, long slow exhale, with a tiny tremor at the end, as if she were recovering from an earlier bout of crying. This perplexed me.

Had she been crying? Had she come to me for comfort?

No. Samantha coming to me for comfort was wishful thinking. She was, in fact, truly sleepwalking.

I considered waking her, but the memory of her earlier admission —about trouble sleeping—kept me in place. I told myself she deserved rest. She deserved peace. If that meant I was her prisoner for a night, then so be it. I would not move until she let me go. It was a very least I could do.

Carefully, gently, I placed my arm around her shoulders and held her there. I wanted to kiss her hair, but did not. I let my lips hover a centimeter away. My cock remained hard, an unyielding iron bar between us. She did not notice.

Time passed. Maybe five minutes. Maybe an hour.

I thought about every moment of our shared history, and every time

I'd failed her, and every way I wanted to make it up to her now. I wondered if she would ever know what she did to me, what she meant to me, if I'd ever get a chance to tell her. If she would one day forgive me.

But then, Samantha shifted, just a little, nuzzling her face deeper into my neck. My eyes closed and I gritted my teeth, commanding myself not to move. She made a sound, a quiet mewling noise, then pressed her nose to my skin and inhaled deeply, as if she were drawing something out of me. Then she stilled again.

Samantha smelled like gardenia and something else, something I could only describe as silky and warm and fucking addictive.

Her hand, still under my shirt, flexed against my stomach, and I realized I held her too tightly. I loosened my grip immediately, worried I might hurt her.

She settled again, head heavy on my bicep, hair tickling my jaw. I memorized each sensation, catalogued every detail. Her breathing grew slower. A wet patch of tears, maybe sweat, formed on my shirt where her face pressed against me.

I would not sleep tonight. I would suffer instead.

But, I reminded myself, suffering with her close seemed so much better than suffering in her absence. This kind of pain, I would pay any price for it. To have her here, in my arms, even for a single night, a luxury I did not deserve.

Oh well. *Lucky me.*

When the sun rose, I would make her coffee, and I would make it strong, and I would never tell her how completely she'd undone me.

I would let her believe it was nothing, no big deal.

And, eventually, I would let her go.

But not yet. Not. . . tonight.

Scan me to receive new book updates and news from Penny!

Scan me if you'd like a signed copy of this or any Penny Reid book!

SNEAK PEEK: FUNDAMENTALS OF BIOLOGY: REPRODUCTION

INTRODUCTION TO EVOLUTIONARY MODELS

Samantha

Sunlight. Actual, golden, warm-on-my-face sunlight. My first coherent thought of the day was, *So, this is what it's like to sleep soundly through the night and wake up after sunrise.* The next was, *I feel fucking awesome.*

For the first time in two years, I was well rested and not fighting a caffeine-withdrawal headache.

Maybe I'd died and this was the afterlife, a high-thread-count sheet, a cocoon of perfect warmth, and a brain empty of intrusive thoughts but full of serotonin, the type only made possible by an appropriate length and number of REM cycles. I allowed myself the decadence of drifting there, savoring the delicate pressure of a memory-foam pillow against my temple, the gentle weight of a duvet across my hips, and the luxurious sense of not having a single place I needed to be.

I let myself enjoy this blissful state for exactly eight seconds before my limbs, traitorous as ever, craved movement. So, I began to stretch, arching my toes. But before I could fully commence a morning starfish, I froze. Because my left hand was palming the undeniable reality of another human being.

There's a microsecond between "that's a person" and "which person" that, for most people, might be raw panic. For me, however, it was pure professionalism. I had a procedure for this.

Step one: Assess level of nudity. My left hand, still frozen mid-stretch, confirmed bare skin, but not below-the-waist bare. Chest, maybe? Arm, maybe? Stomach, *definitely*. And a muscly one.

Step two: Identify the person. Keeping my eyes closed, I mentally replayed the previous twelve hours. Had I gone out? No. Had I let anyone into the building? Also no. Had I, at any point, consumed more than the recommended daily allowance of alcohol? Negative.

So, no hookups. No midnight social calls. No one should be in my bed.

Yet, this warm body next to mine definitely existed. And this wasn't a dream, I wasn't asleep. Someone warm and solid and occupying a scandalous percentage of my mattress.

Step three: Confirm position. With the meticulousness of a bomb technician, I moved my fingertips. Male, for sure. Hairless chest, ridged with muscle. Not moving, which meant asleep or possibly dead. Breath? Yes, regular, slow, and deep. So, not dead. I could feel his chest rise and fall beneath the new position of my left hand.

Step four: Open eyes, assess the scene, and—*oh my God!*

This wasn't the afterlife. This was a penthouse apartment in the Lower East Side of Manhattan.

And I was spooning Andreas Kristiansen.

ABOUT THE AUTHOR

Penny Reid is the *New York Times*, *Wall Street Journal*, and *USA Today* bestselling author of the Winston Brothers and Knitting in the City series. She used to spend her days writing federal grant proposals as a biomedical researcher, but now she writes kissing books. Penny is an obsessive knitter and manages the #OwnVoices-focused mentorship incubator / publishing imprint, Smartypants Romance. She lives in Seattle Washington with her husband, three kids, and dog named Hazel.

Come find me
Mailing List: http://pennyreid.ninja/newsletter/
Email: pennreid@gmail.com …hey, you! Email me ;-)

amazon.com/Penny-Reid/e/B00BI7A7SY

bookbub.com/authors/penny-reid

goodreads.com/ReidRomance

facebook.com/pennyreidwriter

instagram.com/reidromance

patreon.com/smartypantsromance

tiktok.com/@authorpennyreid

x.com/reidromance

OTHER BOOKS BY PENNY REID

<u>Knitting in the City Series</u>

(Interconnected Standalones, Adult Contemporary Romantic Comedy)

<u>Neanderthal Seeks Human: A Smart Romance (#1)</u>

<u>Neanderthal Marries Human: A Smarter Romance (#1.5)</u>

<u>Friends without Benefits: An Unrequited Romance (#2)</u>

<u>Love Hacked: A Reluctant Romance (#3)</u>

<u>Beauty and the Mustache: A Philosophical Romance (#4)</u>

<u>Ninja at First Sight (#4.75)</u>

<u>Happily Ever Ninja: A Married Romance (#5)</u>

<u>Dating-ish: A Humanoid Romance (#6)</u>

<u>Marriage of Inconvenience: (#7)</u>

<u>Neanderthal Seeks Extra Yarns (#8)</u>

<u>Knitting in the City Coloring Book (#9)</u>

<u>Winston Brothers Series</u>

(Interconnected Standalones, Adult Contemporary Romantic Comedy, spinoff of Beauty and the Mustache)

<u>Beauty and the Mustache (#0.5)</u>

<u>Truth or Beard (#1)</u>

<u>Grin and Beard It (#2)</u>

<u>Beard Science (#3)</u>

<u>Beard in Mind (#4)</u>

<u>Beard In Hiding (#4.5)</u>

<u>Dr. Strange Beard (#5)</u>

<u>Beard with Me (#6)</u>

Beard Necessities (#7)

Winston Brothers Paper Doll Book (#8)

<u>Hypothesis Series</u>

(New Adult Romantic Comedy Trilogies)

<u>Elements of Chemistry</u>

ATTRACTION (#1)

HEAT (#2)

CAPTURE (#3)

Laws of Physics

MOTION (#4)

SPACE (#5)

TIME (#6)

Fundamentals of Biology

INHERITANCE (#7)

REPRODUCTION (#8)

EVOLUTION (#9)

<u>Irish Players (Rugby) Series – by L.H. Cosway and Penny Reid</u>

(Interconnected Standalones, Adult Contemporary Sports Romance)

The Hooker and the Hermit (#1)

The Pixie and the Player (#2)

The Cad and the Co-ed (#3)

The Varlet and the Voyeur (#4)

<u>Dear Professor Series</u>

(New Adult Romantic Comedy)

Kissing Tolstoy (#1)

Kissing Galileo (#2)

Ideal Man Series

(Interconnected Standalones, Adult Contemporary Romance Series of Jane Austen Reimaginings)

Pride and Dad Jokes (#1, TBD)

Man Buns and Sensibility (#2, TBD)

Sense and Manscaping (#3, TBD)

Persuasion and Man Hands (#4, TBD)

Mantuary Abbey (#5, TBD)

Mancave Park (#6, TBD)

Emmanuel (#7, TBD)

Handcrafted Mysteries Series

(A Romantic Cozy Mystery Series, spinoff of *The Winston Brothers Series*)

Engagement and Espionage (#1)

Marriage and Murder (#2)

Home and Heist (TBD)

Baby and Ballistics (TBD)

Pie Crimes and Misdemeanors (TBD)

Good Folks Series

(Interconnected Standalones, Adult Contemporary Romantic Comedy, spinoff of *The Winston Brothers Series*)

Totally Folked (#1)

Folk Around and Find Out (#2)

All Folked Up (#3)

Three Kings Series

(Interconnected Standalones, Holiday-themed Adult Contemporary Romantic Comedies)

Homecoming King (#1)

<u>Standalones</u>